W9-AGB-087

LIKE FAMILY

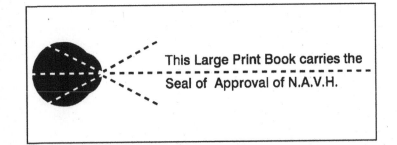

This Large Print Book carries the
Seal of Approval of N.A.V.H.

LIKE FAMILY

PAOLO GIORDANO

English translation by Anne Milano Appel

THORNDIKE PRESS
A part of Gale, Cengage Learning

GALE
CENGAGE Learning·

Farmington Hills, Mich • San Francisco • New York • Waterville, Maine
Meriden, Conn • Mason, Ohio • Chicago

GALE
CENGAGE Learning®

LIBRARY OF CONGRESS CATALOGING-IN-PUBLICATION DATA

Names: Giordano, Paolo, 1982– author. | Appel, Anne Milano, translator.
Title: Like family / by Paolo Giordano ; English translation by Anne Milano Appel.
Other titles: Nero e l'argento. English
Description: Large print edition. | Waterville, Maine : Thorndike Press, 2016. | © 2015 | Series: Thorndike Press large print basic
Identifiers: LCCN 2015047403 | ISBN 9781410488275 (hardcover) | ISBN 1410488276 (hardcover)
Subjects: LCSH: Large type books. | Domestic fiction. | GSAFD: Love stories.
Classification: LCC PQ4907.I57 N4713 2016 | DDC 853/.92—dc23
LC record available at http://lccn.loc.gov/2015047403

Published in 2016 by arrangement with Pamela Dorman Books/Viking, an imprint of Penguin Publishing Group, a division of Penguin Random House LLC

Printed in Mexico
1 2 3 4 5 6 7 20 19 18 17 16

to the girl I'm seeing

There really was a Mrs. A. in my life. She stayed in my house, shared life with my family for a few years, then she had to leave us. This book was inspired by her story. It was meant as a homage to her, a way to keep her with me a little longer. I've changed most of the names and I've changed several details, but not what I felt was the nature of Mrs. A. And, certainly, not what was my feeling toward her.

What does it mean to love some-
body? It is always to seize that
person in a mass, extract him or
her from a group, however small,
in which he or she participates,
whether it be through the family
only or through something else;
then to find that person's own
{wolf} packs, the multiplicities he
or she encloses within himself or
herself which may be of an entirely different nature.

— Gilles Deleuze and Félix
Guattari, *A Thousand Plateaus*

CONTENTS

11

Mrs. A.

On my thirty-fifth birthday, Mrs. A. abruptly gave up the determination that in my eyes characterized her more than any other quality and, already laid out in a bed that by then seemed too big for her body, finally abandoned the world we all know.

That morning I had gone to the airport to pick up Nora, back from a brief business trip. Though it was late December, winter was dragging its feet, and the monotonous stretches at the sides of the highway were whitened by a thin layer of fog, as if to suggest the snow that couldn't make up its mind to fall. Nora answered the phone, after which she didn't say much, just sat there listening. "I see," she said, "all right, Tuesday," and then she added one of those sentences that experience provides us with when there are no adequate words: "Maybe it's better that way."

I pulled off into the first service area to allow her to get out of the car and pace aimlessly around the parking lot by herself. She wept quietly, her right hand clamped over her mouth and nose. Among the countless things I've learned

14

about my wife in ten years of marriage is her habit of isolating herself in times of grief. She suddenly becomes unreachable and won't allow anyone to console her, forcing me to remain a useless spectator to her suffering — a rejection that I sometimes interpreted as a lack of generosity.

For the rest of the way, I drove more slowly; it seemed like a form of respect. We spoke about Mrs. A., recalling some anecdotes from the past, although for the most part they weren't really anecdotes — we didn't know much about her — just routines. Routines so rooted in our family life that to us they seemed almost legendary: the reliability with which she updated us each morning on the horoscope she'd heard on the radio while we were still asleep; her way of taking over certain rooms of the house, especially the kitchen, so that we felt we should ask her permission to open our own refrigerator; the proverbs with which she curtailed what to her were unnecessary complications created by us young people; her military, masculine step and her incorrigible tightfistedness — remember the time we forgot to leave her money for the shopping? She emptied the jar of pennies, scraping up each and every one of the coins.

After a moment or two of silence, Nora added, "What a woman, though! Our Babette. Always there for us. Even this time she waited for me to get back."

I did not point out that she had just summarily excluded me from the overall picture. Nor did I dare confess what I'd been thinking that very same moment: that Mrs. A. had waited for my birthday to leave us. Each of us was thus fabricating a small, personal consolation. There is nothing more we can do when faced with someone's death except devise some extenuating circumstances for it, attributing to the deceased one final gesture of thoughtfulness toward us and arranging the coincidences in some rational order. Yet today, with the inevitable detachment of distance, I have a hard time believing that it was really so. Her suffering had taken Mrs. A. far away from us, from anyone, long before that December morning, leading her to walk alone to a remote corner of the world — just as Nora had walked away from me in the service area on the highway — and from there she'd turned her back on us.

We called her that, Babette. We liked the nickname because it suggested a sense of belonging, and she liked it because it was exclusively hers and sounded precious, with its French cadence. I don't think Emanuele ever understood what it meant; maybe someday he'll come across Karen Blixen's story, or more likely the movie, and then he'll make the connection.

Nonetheless, he accepted that Mrs. A. had become Babette from a certain point on, his Babette, and I suspect that by assonance he associated that nickname with her babouches, the slippers that his nanny put on as soon as she entered our house and replaced side by side next to the chest at the end of the day. When Nora had noticed the worn-down condition of the soles and bought her a new pair, she'd confined them to the closet, never used. That's how she was — she never changed anything. She genuinely opposed change body and soul, and though her obstinacy was funny, even foolish at times, I can't deny we liked it. In our lives, my life and those of Nora and

Emanuele — who at that time seemed to fluctuate each day, swaying precariously in the wind like a young plant — she was a steady element, a haven, an ancient tree with a trunk so massive that even three pairs of arms could not encircle it.

She had become Babette one Saturday in April. Emanuele was already talking, but he was still sitting in the high chair, so it must have been maybe five or six years ago. For months Mrs. A. had been insisting that we go and visit her at her home, at least once, for dinner. Nora and I, experts at declining invitations that even vaguely hinted at family gatherings, had avoided it for quite some time, but Mrs. A.

was not easily discouraged, and every Monday she was prepared to renew the invitation for the following weekend. We gave in. We drove up to Rubiana in a state of unusual concentration, as if gearing up to do something unnatural that would require a high degree of industry. We weren't used to sitting down at the table with Mrs. A., not back then: despite the constant time spent together, an implicitly hierarchical relationship existed between us by which, if anything, she was on her feet, busy, while we ate and talked about our own affairs.

"Rubiana," Nora said with a puzzled look, gazing at the densely wooded hill. "Imagine living here all your life."

We toured the three-room apartment where Mrs. A. spent her lonely widowhood, uttering excessive compliments. The information we had about her past was scant — Nora knew only a little more than I — and since we could not attribute a sentimental significance to what we saw, the setting seemed no more, no less than an unnecessarily pompous home, very clean and a little kitschy. Mrs. A. had set the round table in the living room impeccably, with silverware aligned on a floral tablecloth and heavy, gold-rimmed goblets. The dinner itself, I thought, seemed like a pretext to justify the existence of that good china, which obviously hadn't been used in years.

She seduced us with a menu designed to include a combination of our favorites: a farro and lentil soup, marinated cutlets, fennel au gratin in a very light béchamel sauce and a salad of sunflower leaves that she'd picked herself, very finely chopped and seasoned with mustard and vinegar. I still recall each and every course and the physical sensation of gradually relinquishing my initial rigidity and surrendering to that culinary indulgence.

"Just like Babette!" Nora exclaimed.

"Like who?"

So we told her the story, and Mrs. A. was moved listening to it, envisioning herself as the chef who'd left the Café Anglais to serve the two spinsters and then spent all her money preparing an unforgettable feast for them. She dabbed at her eyes with the edge of her apron and quickly turned away, pretending to be doing something. Years passed before I saw her cry again, and then it was not out of joy but fear. By that time we were familiar enough so that I wasn't embarrassed to take her hand and say, "You can do it. Many people let it beat them, but you know illness because you've already faced it once. You're strong enough."

And I really believed it. Afterward I saw her fall apart so quickly that there wasn't even time to say a proper good-bye, no chance to find

the right words to express what she
had meant to us.

BIRD OF PARADISE
(I)

The end came swiftly, but it had been heralded by an omen, or at least that is what Mrs. A. convinced herself of in the final months, as though a portent could give meaning to what was simply misfortune.

At the tail end of summer, a year and a half prior to her funeral, she is working in the garden behind her apartment building. She is pulling up the now-useless green-bean plants to make room for the savoy cabbage when a bird alights just a few feet away from her, on one of the stones that border her rectangle of property.

Mrs. A., bent over her vegetable plot despite her sixty-eight years, remains motionless so as not to scare it, while the bird peers at her inquisitively. She's never seen one like it. Its size is roughly that of a magpie, but its colors are quite different. Below the head, lemon-yellow plumes extend from the breast, merging with the blue plumage of its back and wings, and it has long white tail feathers, the cottony threads curled at the tips like fishhooks. It does not seem disturbed by her presence; on the contrary, Mrs. A. has the impression that it perched there just so she can admire it. Her heart begins to pound — she can't explain why; her knees nearly give way. She suspects that it may belong to a rare, precious tropical species and that it perhaps escaped from the cage of a collector: there are no specimens of its kind in the Rubiana area. Actually, as far as she knows, there aren't even any bird collectors in Rubiana.

Abruptly the bird tilts its head to one side and begins poking at a wing with its beak. Its movements have something cunning about them. No, not cunning, not really, what's the word . . . ? Haughty, that's it. When it's done preening, its jet-black eyes bore straight into those of Mrs. A. Finally, lifting off the stone without a sound, it takes flight. Mrs. A. follows its trajectory, shading her eyes from the sun with her hand. She would like to keep watching it, but the bird soon disappears among the neighboring oaks.

That night she'd dreamed about the encounter with that parrotlike bird. When she told me about it, she was already quite ill, and at that point it was impossible to distinguish factual elements from those that were imagined or the fruit of simple suggestion. But I think it is true that, in the morning, Mrs. A. looked for a picture of the bird in a book on the fauna of the Val di Susa that she had in her house, because she showed me the book. And it is undoubtedly true that, not finding a picture of it, she decided to go and see a friend, a painter keenly interested in ornithology, because she told me about that visit in detail.

I never understood much about the nature of her relationship with the painter. She was not inclined to talk about it, perhaps out of reserve, because he was a well-known artist — unquestionably the most distinguished person she still saw after Renato passed away — or maybe she was just possessive. I know that she occasionally cooked for him or ran errands for him, but basically she was a kind of lady friend, a companion with whom he could spend time platonically. I have the impression that they saw each other more than she let on. Every Sunday, after Mass, Mrs. A. went to visit him and stayed until dinnertime. The painter's house, its deep red façade hidden behind tall beech trees, was just three minutes away from her apartment by car or ten minutes on foot, along a curved, paved road.

The painter was a midget: she had no qualms about calling him that; indeed she spoke that word with a hint of cruel satisfaction. After so many years, she confessed, she had not stopped having stupid thoughts about him. For example, she had never stopped wondering how it felt never to touch the floor with your feet when sitting down. And she was always looking at his hands, those stubby, somewhat ridiculous fingers, capable of producing wonders. He was the only man whom Mrs. A., barely five foot six, could surpass in height, yet he had such abundant, intense appeal that it was always she who felt surpassed. Spending time with him, sitting in the living room that served as a studio, among the paintings and the picture frames, reminded her of the days when Renato wanted her with him to rummage through cellars and attics in search of some rare, overlooked piece.

"It must have been a hoopoe," he'd guessed that morning in late August.

He was gruff, and lately he'd gotten much worse, but Mrs. A. was used to it and didn't take any notice. At one time, she told me, the house had been a beehive of activity, with gallery owners, friends and models who posed naked coming and going. Now there were only four women who took turns looking after him; they were foreigners, and none of them was beautiful enough to be immortalized on canvas. Mrs. A. knew that the painter spent almost all his time thinking about earlier days, that he hardly painted anymore, that he was alone. Just like her.

"I know very well what a hoopoe looks like. That wasn't what it was," she retorted, annoyed.

With a little hop, the painter got down from his chair and disappeared into the next room. Mrs. A. started looking around the studio, as if she weren't already familiar enough with it. Her favorite painting was there on the floor, unfinished. It depicted a nude woman sitting at a table, her full breasts slightly spread apart, the large nipples a much deeper pink than the surrounding skin. In front of her, four bright rosy peaches and a knife with which she perhaps intends to peel them. But she doesn't. She remains static forever, waiting for the right moment.

"It was his most beautiful painting. And that day he finished it right before my eyes, in half an hour. He said to me, 'You came by car? Then you can take it with you.' He did it out of compassion, I'm sure. If I had asked him for it, he wouldn't have given it to me. But he understood how things were. Before anyone, before the doctors. He knew it because of the bird. He came back into the living room with a leather portfolio and placed it on my lap. 'Is this the one?' he asked. I recognized it immediately, with those long white feathers looped behind. He hadn't seen one in years, since '71 at least. He thought they'd disappeared. But the bird of paradise had come just for me. They call it that, bird of paradise, but it brings bad luck. I told him, 'We're old now, the two

of us. What can bad luck do to us?'
Just think, I had broken a mirror
only a few days before. Oh, but the
painter became furious. 'Never
mind the mirror!' he shouted. 'That
bird brings death!' "

Once I asked Nora if she had ever
seriously believed the story about
the omen. She turned the question
back to me:

"Did you?"

"Of course not."

"Well, obviously I did. I imagine
that will always be a difference
between the two of us."

It was late evening, Emanuele was
asleep, and we were quietly clean-
ing up in the kitchen. We had left a
bottle of wine open on the table,

almost half full.

"What do you miss most about her?" I asked.

Nora didn't need time to think about it; clearly she had already considered the question herself. "I miss the way she encouraged us. People are so stingy with their encouragement. They just want to be sure you're more needy than they are." There was a lingering silence. I can't make up my mind whether her pauses are natural or if she metes them out one by one, like an actress. "Not her," she added, "she was always rooting for us."

"You never told me what you two talked about all the time you spent in bed."

"Did we talk a lot?"

"You sure did."

Nora took a sip of wine from the bottle. She lets herself forget her manners only in the evening, when we're alone, as if exhaustion and intimacy relaxed her inhibitions. A dark red stain remained on her lips.

"She was the one who did the talking," she said. "I listened. She told me about Renato. She made him central to every conversation, as if he were still alive. I'm sure she talked out loud to him when she was home alone. She confessed that she still set the table for him after all those years. I always thought it was very romantic. Romantic and a little pathetic. But everything that's very romantic is also pathetic, isn't it?"

We would have conversations like that almost every night, Nora and I, especially in the first few months following Mrs. A.'s death. It was a strategy that we had honed so as not to succumb to any uncertainties: returning to them over and over again, until it seemed that nothing but crystal-clear air came out of our mouths. Mrs. A. was the only real witness of the enterprise we embarked on day after day, the sole observer of the bond that held us together, and when she talked about Renato, it was as if she wanted to suggest something that had to do with us, to pass along the instructions for a relationship that had been perfect and pure, albeit doomed and brief. In the long run, every love needs someone to witness and acknowledge it, to validate it, or it may turn out to be just a mirage. Without her gaze we felt at risk.

Nonetheless, we were late getting to the funeral. We were ready on time, but then we got sidetracked by some stupid little tasks, almost as if what awaited us was just one more job among many we had to see to. Emanuele was particularly restless and constantly asking questions about what "going to heaven" meant exactly and why it was impossible for a person ever to come back. They were questions to which he knew the answers, an excuse to voice his excitement (his first funeral: isn't that, too, just a source of wonder for a child?), but we didn't feel much inclined to play along. We ignored him.

On the way the disintegration of the family continued. Nora accused me of taking the longer route, and I started naming the pointless tasks she'd dawdled over before we left the house: putting on her makeup, for example, as though one had to show up at a funeral wearing makeup. If Mrs. A. had been there with us, she would have chosen one of her proverbs and put an end to it, but she was waiting for us at the ceremony, resting in the pine box, speechless.

We entered the church with some embarrassment; there were more people gathered there than I had expected. I heard little of the homily, worried as I was about the car, which I'd hastily parked along a narrow side street. I imagined a vehicle, one of those buses that serve the province, stuck there waiting for us, the passengers having gotten off, wondering who the idiot was who had blocked them in there, but I couldn't make up my mind to go out and check. We skipped the final farewells, since our presence could console no one and perhaps because we thought we ourselves had a right to be consoled.

Emanuele wanted to follow the

coffin to the grave site. We thought it was a whim, foolish curiosity, so we didn't agree. A burial is not something for a child, and that one in particular wasn't something for us. There are situations that should be left to the intimacy of family and close friends, and who were we to Mrs. A.? Employers, not much more than that. Death realigns roles according to a formal order of importance, instantly mending the sentimental rules that one allowed oneself to break in life, and it didn't matter much that Emanuele was the closest thing to a grandson that Mrs. A. had known or that she'd liked to consider us, Nora and me, her adoptive children. We were not.

ORPHANS

It was her natural, nearly religious inclination to look after people that brought her to us in the beginning. When Nora's pregnancy had proved unlike the marvelous experience we had envisioned and the fetus had begun squirming to get out at twenty-four weeks, we asked for Mrs. A.'s help, having learned that she was free since the day my father-in-law realized he could get by without domestic assistance. With my wife confined to bed, I

had to show Mrs. A. around the house myself, doing my best to explain details that I wasn't very familiar with: where to pour the fabric softener and the detergent, how to replace the vacuum-cleaner bags and how often to water the plants on the balcony. Less than halfway through the tour, Mrs. A. interrupted me. "Go ahead, go! Go on, don't worry about a thing."

In the evening, back from work, I'd find her sitting at Nora's bedside like a guard dog, ears pricked. They'd be chatting, but Mrs. A. had already slipped on her rings and pinned the brooch on her cardigan, and her coat was settled on her shoulders. When she saw me, she'd get up with the energy of

someone who wasn't tired in the least, then lead me into the kitchen to explain what dishes she had cooked for dinner, how to reheat them so they wouldn't dry out and where to put the dirty pots and pans afterward. "Don't bother washing them. I'll do it tomorrow," she'd always add. At the beginning I disobeyed her, but when I saw that in the morning she redid the dishes I'd washed anyway, I gave in to her command.

Such perfection could be irritating at times, and she herself hard to bear, with all her convictions and sensible but not-very-original pronouncements. Nora, having spent a good part of her day with Mrs. A., often vented her frustration at be-

ing trapped in bed for weeks by taking it out on her. "She's an exasperating woman!" she complained. "Exasperating and especially pedantic!"

The period during which we put ourselves in the care of another person — care we doubted we'd ever encounter or deserve again — was also the period when we came up with the first subterfuges to evade it.

There was a restaurant where Nora and I went from time to time — not a real restaurant, actually, just a fish market that at night set some tightly packed tables with tablecloths and plastic forks and served fried fish in aluminum trays. We'd stumbled onto it when we were just married, and since then it had become our spot. Prior to venturing forth with my wife to that out-of-the-way corner, crustaceans and mollusks hadn't appealed to me at all (before Nora, I didn't like a lot of things), but I loved watching her eat them. I loved the concentration she applied to peeling the shrimp and then offering me half and insisting that I take it, I loved the way she dug the sea snails out of their shells and how she sucked her moist fingertips between one course and another. The fish market, until it closed recently — leaving us deprived of another secondary but essential point of reference — was the scene of our most intimate, tribal rituals. Important discussions, momentous announcements, toasts to secret anniversaries — all took place there. Whenever we left, Nora's hair and our clothes would reek of grease; we carried that smell into the house with us, as if to seal decisions we'd made, truths we'd come to.

Mrs. A. wouldn't allow Nora, in her condition, to eat even just a mouthful of "that garbage," as she called it, frowning like a customs officer as she inspected the contents of the take-out meal that I'd picked up at the fish market. "And you either," she added, pointing her finger at me. "I already made a meat loaf."

She bundled up forty euros' worth of fried fish and personally made sure that it ended up in the Dumpster down the street.

We learned to con her. When Nora showed an irresistible craving for batter-fried cuttlefish and calamari, I secretly visited our restaurant, then kept the package hidden in the car until Mrs. A. left. So as not to arouse suspicion, we threw a suitable portion of the dinner she had prepared for us in the trash.

"Will she notice the fried-food smell?" Nora fretted, so I made the rounds of the rooms spraying citrus deodorizer, while she implored me not to make her laugh because she'd go into labor.

"Let me see if you have bits of shrimp between your teeth!" I ordered her.

"It's not like she checks my mouth!"

"That woman sees everything."

Then I kissed her on the lips and slipped a hand into her neckline to feel the warmth under her nightgown. Together we searched out shadowy recesses where we could hide from Babette's omnipresent gaze, which from above lit up everything like the sun at its zenith.

By the time Emanuele was born, we were too spoiled to give up her attentions. Mrs. A. went from being Nora's nurse to being our son's nanny, as if there were a natural continuity between the two occupations, and although she had not cared for a newborn baby before that, she immediately proved to have very clear ideas — much clearer than ours — on what to do and what not to do.

Her pay cut into the family budget, but not as much as it could have: she did not keep an exact accounting of the time she devoted to us, nor did we ever agree on an hourly rate. On Fridays she accepted without protest a sum that we considered appropriate, which Nora calculated based on a mysterious, extremely flexible schedule. Every weekday morning for over eight years, Mrs. A. showed up at our door, ringing the bell before opening with her bunch of keys, lest she catch us in a private moment. Sometimes she'd already done the shopping and would immediately hand us the receipt, standing there, not moving, until we reimbursed her for the full amount.

On Emanuele's first day of kindergarten, Nora and I were present, and so was Mrs. A. On the first day of elementary school, however, only two relatives per child were allowed, and I had to stay outside. When someone mistakenly referred to Babette as his "grandmother," Emanuele did not correct her. Mrs. A. felt she held our child's delicate heart in her hands, and indeed she did.

You can imagine our disappointment, therefore, our bewilderment, when in early September of 2011, when we needed her more than ever to plan for the return to school, Mrs. A. announced her firm intention not to come anymore.

"May I ask why?" Nora asked her, more annoyed than sorry to hear it at that moment. There are rules, after all, to be followed regarding work: giving notice, letters of resignation sent by mail, keeping one's word.

"Because I'm tired," Mrs. A. said, but from her tone she seemed bitter if anything.

The call ended very quickly: eight years of working together — one might almost say living together — dismissed with the vague excuse of being tired.

■ ■ ■ ■

She really doesn't show up any-more. Of the three of us, Emanuele is the only one who has not yet learned that nothing lasts forever when it comes to human relation-ships. He is also the only one who doesn't know that this is not neces-sarily a disadvantage. Still, in this specific situation, having to tell him that, out of the blue, his nanny has decided not to look after him any-more, it's hard to see the advanta-geous aspects, so Nora and I stall for time. After a week it's he who asks, "When is Babette coming?"

"For the moment she can't come. Go put your pajamas on now."

Yet we, too, hurt and terrified at

the thought that running the household has suddenly fallen upon us, ask ourselves what really happened, where we could have gone wrong. We talk about it endlessly, like a couple of orphans. Finally we pinpoint what we see as the most likely cause of Mrs. A.'s mutiny. About ten days prior to her notice, a handwritten note in block letters had appeared on our building's buzzer panel. The woman who rents the garage space next to ours was asking the careless driver who had nearly bashed in the electric door to step forward and give himself up. The sign had been left there to curl up in the wind, ignored. Nora had sworn to me that she'd had nothing to do with it, knowing

full well she was high on the list of
suspects, not only because of the
arrangement of the parking spaces
but because of her irreverent, often
out-of-control driving. The only
one who used the parking garage
besides us was Mrs. A. So as not to
waste piles of coins in the parking
meter each day, she took advantage
of the space that I left vacant in the
morning. I had asked her if by
chance she had been the one to
crash into our neighbor's garage
door — it could have happened, it
certainly wasn't anything serious,
and in any case I would take care
of the damage. She had barely
turned around. "Of course it wasn't
me. She must have done it herself,
that one. With that big car she

drives around in."

"That must be it!" Nora says, convincing herself and me both about the version we just came up with. We're lying in bed, eleven o'clock at night. "Naturally that's what happened. You know how touchy she is."

"This suggests that she really was the one who bashed in the garage door."

But Nora silences me. "What do we care about the door? We have to call her."

So the next morning, during a break in the group-theory exercise in which, judging by my students' glazed looks, I was more confusing than usual, I call Mrs. A. I extend an apology for the accusatory, indelicate way in which I addressed her, assuring her that if that's the reason she doesn't want to work for us anymore, I understand, but that we are all eager to make amends. I refer to Emanuele and how much he misses her.

"The garage has nothing to do with it," she cuts me short. "I'm worn out, I already told you."

It is toward the end of that phone call, when we are about to say good-bye somewhat sullenly, that I hear her cough for the first time. She coughs in a way that's different from how you cough when the seasons change. She coughs sharply, gasping for breath, as if someone were playing around, snapping his fingers at the mouth of her trachea.

"What's wrong?" I ask her.

"This cough. It won't go away."

"Have you seen a doctor?"

"No, but I will. I will."

INSOMNIA

Mrs. A.'s defection is soon visible in our house, made clear by multiple signs of neglect, in particular on Nora's desk. The stacks of paper whose loftiness had already been defying the height of medieval towers now reach alarming altitudes, toppling over one another to form a single disordered heap. Some important ones must certainly be hidden in there: bills to pay, notices from Emanuele's school, phone numbers that Nora insists on jotting on Post-its and decorating plans that will cause her to have a mild nervous breakdown when the clients call for them and they can't be found. Not that Mrs. A. ever laid a hand on the documents — better yet, she pretended not to — but often, after she had straightened out the piles so that she could clean, the envelope that my wife had spent days looking for miraculously reappeared: Mrs. A. would leave it on top of the others, as if it just happened to be there.

"They've contacted me about fixing up a chalet in Chamois," Nora says one Sunday afternoon. She's talking loudly to be heard above the roar of the vacuum cleaner she's angrily pushing over an area that doesn't seem to need it. "It's a good job. It would be a good job. Too bad I'll have to turn it down."

"Turn it down? Why?"

"Why? Just look at how things are! I don't have time to breathe, let alone be able to carry out a project in Valle d'Aosta. You see those magazines on the couch? They've been sitting there all morning. I intended to read them, but I won't be able to." She ventures too far from the wall — with a snap the vacuum cleaner's cord detaches from the outlet. The sudden silence startles her. She goes on staring at the magazines. "And there are articles in them that interest me," she says. "They really interest me."

■ ■ ■ ■

We ask her mother to help out. She comes a few times, grudgingly. When she enters the house, she goes through a series of propitiatory rituals: she makes a cup of coffee that she then sips drifting between the balcony and the kitchen, insisting someone keep her company, meanwhile sucking on a cigarette; then she pins up her hair, takes a pair of gloves and a clean apron and puts them on in front of the mirror, studying the effect. Transformed into the perfect domestic helper, she turns to her daughter. "So . . . what needs to be done?"

At that point Nora loses her patience. "*Everything* needs to be done, can't you see?"

They argue so heatedly that her mother quickly leaves the house, offended. After less than a month, we stop asking her to come, and she doesn't offer to return.

A brief experience with an au pair doesn't work out any better. Nora finds her slow and apathetic; she complains that the girl doesn't know Italian well enough to understand her instructions and that she has no sense of order.

"And she looks at you."

"She looks at me?"

"She's got a crush on you, it's obvious."

"You're crazy."

"That's why she does those things

to spite me, like when she broke the teapot. She knew I was particularly fond of it. I'm not saying that she did it on purpose. Not really. It was a kind of subliminal disrespect."

I keep telling her that we'll find someone eventually, we just have to keep looking, but Nora is hardly listening.

"No. We won't find anyone," she murmurs to herself, "no one decent. No one like her."

While my wife vents her dismay during the day, in increasingly bitter and erratic ways, I hold back until night — another difference that has always distinguished us (since I've known her, Nora's ability to sleep is a perpetual miracle). My insomnia has not been so acute since the days of my doctorate, when I accepted the fact that there was a four- or five-hour difference between the rest of the city's bio-rhythms and mine, as if I lived alone on a meridian in the middle of the Atlantic Ocean or had a job that involved night shifts. In recent years the disorder had moderated to little more than a nuisance to be managed judiciously, worsening slightly between seasons. Now, however, I reach a new alarming regularity: every night I wake up at exactly three o'clock and lie there for hours, sometimes until dawn, staring at the subtle play of light on the windows. Whereas at the time of my doctorate I could make up for some of the lost sleep, now, with Emanuele and my classes, the alarm is set for seven-thirty; the sleep deficit builds up, and that's that.

To keep my anxieties at bay, I mentally continue the calculations that I'd left in midstream that afternoon. I'd like to get up, look for a piece of paper and a pencil to jot down my ideas, but I don't dare. Nora forbade me to work at night ever since I confessed that if I do, numbers, letters and functions continue to dance before my eyes, making things worse. During my enforced vigils, I caress my wife's hip in the hope that she will open her eyes for a moment at least.

These are also times when I happen to think of Mrs. A. and feel a sense of loss, of sadness.

As a child I, too, had a nanny. Her name was Teresa, "Teresina" to us, and she lived across the river. I don't remember much about her; I don't recall, for example, ever having touched her or hugged her, nor do I recall her smell. People have lots of sensory memories, comforting, warm memories to return to, but not me: I easily erase whatever isn't visual. I can call to mind only a few fragments about Teresa, like the way she cut up the potatoes she fried, in wedges, without peeling them first. I can also remember her stockings, opaque brownish hose whose thickness did not vary from one season to another. But the clearest episode concerning her, the one that displaced the others, goes back to the last time I saw her. By then I was in high school, and my mother decided that we had to give up the afternoon to go and call on my nanny. We went to see her at her row-house flat that I had visited many years earlier and of which I had no distinct recollection. It now seemed shabby, vaguely seedy to me. Teresina shared the four rooms with her son's family and spent her days in an armchair from which she kept an eye on her hyperactive granddaughter, who cavorted around and sometimes jumped on her, like a macaque. So my parents had chosen someone poor to look after me: I don't know why, but at that moment the revelation left me indignant. After exchanging pleasantries, we sat for a while, listening to her rasping breath. When we were about to leave, Teresina drew a bill out of her wallet, as if adhering to an old automatic reflex, and insisted that I take it. I was appalled, but, correctly interpreting my mother's look, I accepted it.

I wonder what train of memories Emanuele will have of Mrs. A. when he is grown. There will be a lot fewer of them than I imagine, most likely. In any case, I mull it over, kicking off the covers for the umpteenth time and finally settling on a compromise (one leg in and the other out); I'm certainly not going to suggest he see her. When a relationship is severed, it's best if it's severed cleanly and permanently.

Nora attributes the return of my insomnia to my work and only that. My contract with the university expires in a little over a year, and as of now there's been no talk of renewing it. When I inquired, asking my supervisor about the position that the department has been promising to offer for years, he spread his arms. "What can I tell you? We're waiting for one of the old ones to die. But those guys are hardy."

He did not add anything more, nor was he sensibly tempted, being sixty-six himself, to include himself in the "hardy" group. He doesn't care to dwell too much on the matter of my professional advancement; he finds it more pleasurable to ramble on about departmental intrigues and from there shift to politics in general. Sometimes he goes on like that until nine or ten o'clock at night, when the corridors empty out and the guards lock the doors, except for one side door that opens with a magnetic key card (and if by chance you've forgotten it, you're in big trouble). For the most part, I nod, scribbling out a page of calculations. I'm his personal audience, and I have no choice. I don't think he's happy for us to spend so many hours together either — he always goes away irritated — but he likes to exercise the authority he has over me, and sequestering me in his office is still better than what's waiting for him at home. He's never explained why, but when talking about marriage he becomes more caustic than usual. When I told him that I was getting married, his comment was nearly as callous as what Nora's father said to her: "The important thing is to keep separate accounts, because love is love, but money is money." What my supervisor told me was, "It's still a few months off. You have time to reconsider." He came to the reception alone, stationed himself near the buffet table to make sure he didn't miss any goodies and was among the last to leave, somewhat tipsy. I was told he didn't say a word about the wedding the following morning; instead he complained about something in the food that made him sick.

His ironic statement about the elderly professors will have to be enough for me to defer, for a few months, my fear of finding myself unemployed. Nevertheless, I record the variation in the probability distribution of my academic future, the standing altered by a few decimals in favor of a move to another city, another country — or maybe a dignified surrender, to finally undertake a less noble plan.

■ ■ ■ ■

The hypothesis involving a foreign move has the ability to upset the family's equilibrium. Every time I tell Nora about a research center where a group of young scientists are working in a field related to mine and producing "something really interesting," whenever I reveal to her how working with my supervisor is eroding invisible parts of me and describe the benefit I would gain from getting out from under his influence (being able to sleep again at night, I'm sure of it), her face darkens. She offers a distracted murmur of assent while the silence she counters with immediately afterward implores me not to go any further.

The period in which we learned of her pregnancy was also the time when the move to Zurich, where I had won a four-year research grant, seemed like a definite decision. I was to precede Nora by a few months to allow her to give birth in Italy, and as soon as the baby's documents were obtained, we would all three of us settle in the most alien canton of alien Switzerland. We made an on-site visit together to look for an apartment. We visited three in the same district, the area where the majority of physicists land because it guarantees an acceptable balance between the new salary and the rent, and because there is a movie theater.

Nora barely entered the houses. She nodded mechanically to the real-estate agent and stroked an as-yet-invisible baby bump.

Caught between her strange apathy and my own insecurity, I began pressing her once we'd completed the rounds. So which one did she prefer? Wasn't it better to give up some square footage for a small courtyard, in anticipation of when the child would begin walking? I listed the pros and cons of each option. She listened to me without saying a word. When she spoke, she did so calmly. "I can't live with the smell of Indian food permeating the stairs. I can't live on that carpet, nor on those marbleized floors. And I don't want to go walking through these streets with our child. By myself."

Her eyes filled up, but she didn't cry. "I'm spoiled, I know. And I'm very sorry."

Nonetheless, the plan remained standing for a few weeks, even after Nora was confined to bed and as Mrs. A. was already busying herself around our house, tactfully imposing her new order on our rooms and routines. "Who knows what garbage they eat up there?" she would comment whenever I dared bring up life in Zurich (many of Mrs. A.'s considerations began and ended with food; she viewed meals as the culmination of her days). I'm certain that she and Nora had discussed the move in detail and had already rejected it, though they merely hinted at it with a cunning that was totally feminine. Nora often exercises that kind of forcefulness in matters that concern us, consisting of a firm but gentle opposition: she enacts her will, bit by bit. With a spirit not unlike that with which she furnishes other people's homes, she has also furnished my life, which before her was bare and unadorned.

Both women waited for me to grasp their decision, and then they granted me the benefit of formally making my own. One morning I wrote an e-mail in which I explained in just a few lines that due to complications in my wife's pregnancy I was forced to give up my grant. My supervisor was scornful of such surrender. "Scientific discoveries are not fond of convenient lives, much less inconvenient wives," he said. In actuality he was glad about my renunciation, since no one else would have quickly taken over the work that I did for him (the development of dozens of Feynman diagrams, substituting for him in the group-theory course, drafting clean copies of his notes, the numerical simulations that I had to run in the evening and check in the middle of the night — all the things that enabled him to poke around on the Internet most of the time and only rarely show off at the blackboard in his office, displaying how smoothly the algebra, in all its brazen beauty, flowed from the chalk he held).

That evening, however, descending the stairs in the institute's most modern wing, I, too, felt an unexpected relief, even a sense of gallantry, for how I had set aside my own ambitions in support of Nora's serenity. My emigrant colleagues might have academic glory unlocked to them and spacious offices in glass-and-metal structures, but they would live far away, far off not only from here but far off from anywhere. They would meet and marry foreign women, "convenient wives," for the most part Nordic, with whom they would communicate in an intermediary language, French or English, like diplomats.

And I? I, on the other hand, had Nora, who understood every nuance of the words I uttered and every implication of those I chose not to say. Could I aspire to anything more than that or imagine risking it all for a grant, albeit a prestigious one? All progress made by physics from the beginning — heliocentrism and Newton's law of universal gravitation; Maxwell's synthetic, perfect equations and Planck's constant; restricted and general relativity; multidimensional twisted strings and the most remote pulsars — all the glory of those discoveries taken together would not be enough to give me the same sense of satisfaction. I was mindful of the fact that romantic ecstasy was destined to last just a brief time (not Planck's constant — that would remain forever), and I had enough experience in relationships to know that such bliss could just as quickly turn into its exact opposite — but for that evening at least I could cling to it. Returning home, I deviated from the shortest route and at the fish market bought enough fried fish to feed a family of four. There was never another mention of Zurich.

And now here we are again. I'm back to speculating about European destinations that might reconcile my professional needs with Nora's expectations and which at least have an Italian elementary school for Emanuele. Durham, Mainz, Uppsala, Freiburg — none of them meet all the criteria completely, so I cross them off in succession. When I finish that list, I move on to a different one: the names of the colleagues with whom I'll be competing for the next research grant. I check out their recent work on the Net, the number of citations they've gathered, I enter the data into an app and calculate the scores to compare them with mine. I have good reason to believe — with a few points in my favor, assuming the estimate is correct and excluding departmental intrigues — that I can still make it through at the next round.

Even if that's so, the same uncertainty will come up again in a few years, then yet again, until a stroke of luck appears (a well-timed series of broken femurs on the fifth floor of the physics faculty, for instance) or until, more likely, I decide to put aside an impractical dream and devote my energies to something more concrete. There are positions open in finance, software, business consulting: physicists are able to manage large quantities of information, they are versatile, and above all they do not complain — so they say.

I push further for commiseration from my psychotherapist and declare myself depressed, or at least about to be. He, after describing my depression as "at most theoretical," prescribes ordinary Lexotan for the worst nights.

Here we are, then, all three of us absorbed by ourselves and no one else: Nora reeling from her proliferation of chores, Emanuele trying to suppress his longing for his nanny and me giving in to psychic weakness. A family just starting out is sometimes like that: a nebula of self-centeredness in danger of imploding.

All of this is enough to make me forget Mrs. A.'s cough, which in the meantime has worsened to the point of not allowing her to sleep. Another insomniac, and not because her room is infested with ghosts — her ghosts have been her best friends for a long time — now every time she lies down, her chest begins to heave, until she's forced to sit up again and gulp some more water, more cough syrup.

She's also stopped going to Mass because she was disturbing people; she noticed how they began eyeing her with disapproval, how the shoulders of those in front twitched impatiently. On the last Sunday, she left a few moments before the Eucharist, awkwardly stepping on the foot of the person beside her as she made her way out of the pew. The coughing echoed against the high, unadorned vault, unbearably amplified.

On her walk home via the short-cut that runs through the birch trees, driven by anger, she wondered about the business regarding Communion ("business" is a word that comes to me when talking about her, since she used it so frequently: "a fine business" or "what is this business?" or "we have to settle the business about the socks" — she had a "business" for everything). She wondered whether the special mystique surrounding Communion wasn't a lot of hype after all, dependent on the hymns, the words whispered by the officiant, the people lined up with bowed heads, hands folded in prayer. With that thought, Mrs. A. began slowly to break away from a faith that she had never doubted and that she could have used now more than ever. She would no longer go to confession, not even as the end approached. At a certain point, I think, she was convinced that this time it was up to the Lord to ask *her* for forgiveness.

In fact, one of the rare disagreements between us had to do with religion. For a while she had made up her mind to teach Emanuele some prayers, not paying much attention to our opinion. Not that Nora and I were totally against it, but we'd chosen to get married in a civil ceremony and we had never set foot in a church together, except for other people's ceremonies or purely as tourists. For the sake of conformity, I had received the sacrament of baptism at twelve years of age, along with my First Communion and confirmation, in a kind of convenient three-in-one (my father, who didn't at all agree with it, had gone to the priest with his hand rigidly outstretched and muttered something about Galileo's recantation and the stake, causing the cleric to turn pale). As suddenly as it had appeared, my faith was soon spent.

Nora, more simply, has always been lukewarm with regard to God. As far as I am aware, she never prays and has worn an ebony rosary around her neck for as long as I've known her, oblivious to its symbolic import, just because she likes the way it looks. "What harm is there?" she replied when I seemed puzzled by such an insouciant attitude.

Emanuele seemed to sniff out our ambivalence. At the table he would start reciting Mrs. A.'s prayers, defying us with his eyes. We went on eating, as if we hadn't noticed. When he didn't stop, Nora told him gently but firmly that it was not the proper time, that he should save his prayers for when he was alone in bed.

I wonder if faith would seriously have taken root in our son if Mrs. A. had had more time to nurture it. Maybe it would have been a good thing for him: any kind of belief, rational or not, complex or simple depending on the need, is still better than none, I'd say. Often I have the feeling that those of us educated in the field of rigid consistency, fenced in by scientific rigor, struggle more than others. Maybe Mrs. A. was right to place her trust in the divine to some degree, just as she relied on the radio's morning horoscope. Maybe Nora is right to wear her rosary around her neck so casually.

In a few months, Emanuele's Catholicism vanished. During Mrs. A.'s funeral, I watched him: he couldn't even keep up with the Our Father — he didn't know the words — and he struggled to latch onto scattered bits and pieces, scanning around. Jesus will likely remain just one of many stories that have been told to him.

■ ■ ■ ■

We learned of Mrs. A.'s worsening
condition through a phone call. It's
Nora who calls her one evening. In
all those years, Babette has never
once dialed the number of our
home; I suspect she always paid a
fixed rate on her phone bill and not
a penny more. Nora has a hard
time understanding what she says,
since Mrs. A. is constantly interrupted by her coughing. She first
went to her general doctor, who
prescribed a cortisone inhaler, but
it didn't do any good. So she
wasted fifteen precious days. She
went back, and this time he made
an emergency referral to a pulmonologist, who first ordered an X-ray

and then, when he'd seen that, a CT scan with a contrast medium.

"A CT scan?" Nora asks, alarmed, drawing my attention as well.

A CT scan, yes, but the report hasn't yet arrived. With the X-ray, however, she'd reversed her route. After the pulmonologist, who pointed out a thickening on the right side — "it could be an infection, the start of bronchial pneumonia or bleeding, call it a shadow for the moment" — she went back to her general doctor, the only one who always speaks plainly to her and who did so on this occasion as well. The doctor held the plate up in front of him for a long time, studying it against the light from the window. Then he handed it back to her, rubbed his eyelids with the palms of his hands and said simply, "I wish you the best of luck."

With that, Mrs. A. bursts into uncontrollable tears. CT scan or no CT scan, she knows. As Nora, teary and wide-eyed, forms the letter *C* with her fingers, a capital *C* for "Cancer," mouthing the other letters and then pointing to her chest, Mrs. A., in a paroxysm of coughing and sobbing, rants about a bird that came to find her, a bird that, at the end of the summer, had brought her the seemingly fatal pronouncement.

LA LOCANDIERA

The diagnosis is quickly made. No surprise for Mrs. A., nor for us at that point, though there is a certain amount of bewilderment. Among all cancers, lung cancer is by far the most easily attributable to lifestyle, to pernicious habits, to negligent behavior. Mrs. A. never smoked a cigarette in her life, not even as a young girl when she helped out her father in the tobacco shop; if an impatient customer lit one while still inside the store, she would open the back door to get rid of the stink. There is no significant incidence of malignancies in her family — a great-aunt with throat cancer, a second cousin with a pancreatic tumor — and her personal medical history is limited to an osteoarthritic condition and the usual childhood diseases. She followed a healthy diet; whenever she could, she ate vegetables from her own garden, she breathed clean air and never failed to stick to her regimen, ever. And still.

I convey what I am able to understand of the pathology report to a doctor friend after Mrs. A. reads it to me, mangling all the medical terms (something she will continue to do until the end, her intelligence mocked by the impenetrable scientific jargon, although in the final months she will speak with the assurance of one who feels she has mastered the complexity of internal medicine, having come to know it intimately). I manage to make out "carcinoma" and "non-small-cell" and "stage four," and that is enough for my friend to mutter grimly and say, "It will be quick. They are remarkably swift tumors."

In the flurry of phone calls that follow — we now call her every evening for updates — the words that recur most frequently are "I can't understand it." I'd like to tell her that there is precious little to understand, that it's just the way it is. Her tumor can be classified as a statistic, maybe in the overlooked tail end of a Gaussian curve, though still within the natural order of things, but I keep this realism to myself, expressing it only to Nora, who, like Mrs. A., dazedly wonders why. As far as Nora is concerned, my rationality is only an embellished form of cynicism, one of the things that irritates her the most about me, a residue of my youthful callousness that she has not yet been able to correct. We don't talk about it anymore.

The plausible reason that everyone was looking for arrived soon enough, however, in the form of a newspaper clipping that Giulietta, a neighbor of Mrs. A., brings her one afternoon. A scientific study of dubious credibility has drawn attention to an anomalous percentage of tumors in Val di Susa. Possible causes include the telephone repeater whose noxious effect the residents of the valley have been clamoring about for years and the nuclear power plants along the Rhône.

"Could be," I comment on the phone, "yes, it could be," yet I can't help but note that expressions such as "anomalous" and "nuclear power plants" are perceived by Mrs. A. as reassuring or appalling depending on her need. There's no reason to make an issue of it. The telephone repeater and the trans-border power plants — if that's what it takes, so be it, let's blame them. It's easier to point the finger at enriched uranium in France or electromagnetic radiation than accuse an equally invisible fate, a void, the merciless scourge of God.

Soon there isn't even time to wonder about the reasons. Mrs. A. is overwhelmed by a host of new routines, which starkly remind her of Renato's years of dialysis, only now the body in the spotlight is hers, and she herself is caring for it. With the first cycle of chemotherapy coming up — the oncologist has planned for three of them, with twenty-day intervals, after reluctantly ruling out the idea of an operation — Mrs. A. would like to acquire a wig. She has no way of knowing when her hair will begin to fall out, clump after clump, and she wants to be prepared. By some perversity of fate, her hair is the only feature she really cares about: she walks lopsidedly, she hasn't bought a new dress for at least twenty years (so that we can never go wrong by giving her a cardigan on every birthday), she doesn't spend as much as a penny on cosmetics, and the pieces of jewelry she wears are the same ones her husband knew, but she pays special attention to her hair. Sometimes, to pamper her, Nora would make an appointment with her own hairdresser for Mrs. A. She pointed out to me several times how few women there are whose hair is naturally white like that of Mrs. A., a chalk white streaked with silvery strands. "I hope mine will be like that when I get old," she says, and I suspect that behind that wish there's a deeper longing to identify.

"First I want to get it cut," Mrs. A. announces over the phone, "short, like I wore it when I was a girl. At least I'll get used to seeing myself bald."

Nora takes the idea for what it is, an impulse. "Don't be silly. It suits you the way it is."

The hope left unspoken by Mrs. A. is that cutting her hair will strengthen the roots enough so that it won't fall out anymore. Her way of thinking is cluttered with popular beliefs that always amused or enraged me, depending. She has no idea of the destructive power of the poison that will be introduced into her body, the force with which it will wipe out all forms of life and resistance, good or bad, without differentiating, like a hurricane. Nora finally manages to dissuade her. She takes the trouble to find the best store to shop for a wig. She consults a client for whom she decorated an apartment in Liguria, a woman who the year before sacrificed both breasts to a malignant cyst and of whom Nora now speaks with a certain admiration, as if that experience had promoted the lady to a higher level of consciousness. The woman refers us to a shop in the city center, and, judging from my preliminary phone call, she has not steered us wrong: the girl who answers the phone is much less embarrassed than I am to talk about wigs for a woman with cancer — in fact, she isn't embarrassed at all, as if people called her all the time with the same pressing need.

Mrs. A. comes to our house, and in the kitchen I measure the circumference of her head with the tape measure that was kept in the sewing box, once her exclusive domain. Then I take photos, front, back and profile. The wig will have to be styled just like that forever, a perpetual coiffure for hair that will never grow.

I take her to the fitting myself, which makes me feel rather weird,

almost how I'd feel if I had to ac-
company her to the gynecologist.
Mrs. A. is jovial — cancer can be
defeated — and she seems to be
pleased that this part of the day is
entirely given over to her, that
someone has taken the trouble to
drive her car and now even offers
her a coffee. No one has devoted
any time to her for as long as she
can remember.

Inside the shop they have us take
a seat in a corridor from which you
can keep an eye on what's going
on in the other rooms. Above us
hangs a drop-crystal chandelier fitted with energy-saving bulbs. The
ambience of the place falls some-
where between elegant and shabby,
though more shabby, actually.

Mrs. A. points out the pieces of furniture, naming the style for each one: Empire, Liberty, Baroque . . . "See how many things I could have taught a child?" She sighs. But the child never arrived.

When Nora and I kissed for the first time, we were both wearing wigs: hers about a foot high, shaped like a pineapple, mine with curly gray ringlets. We both had white makeup on our faces. We were in acting class, rehearsing some scenes from *La locandiera,* none of which would be performed in front of an audience. We dressed in costumes to enhance the experience.

Every evening the male students and doctoral candidates in the department of physics, myself included, left the austere building on Via Giuria and scattered throughout the city looking for places where there were girls who did not have the same mortifying sobriety in their dress, the same slipshod disregard for their bodies in general. We took courses in photography, Asian languages, cooking, tango and aerobics; we slipped into film-club discussions full of female modern-lit students or pretended to believe in the spiritual potential of kundalini yoga, all to open the door to sex. After several such ventures, I'd landed in the acting class, though I had no interest in theater. At the first session, Nora, who had been studying for over a year, led me through the breathing exercises. My wife-to-be violently shoved her hand into my abdomen, forcing me to emit an embarrassing, spontaneous sound, before she'd even told me her name.

After class, late that evening, we walked back and forth along the riverfront, orbiting around the stop where a bus would eventually split us up and letting more than one of them go by. Most of the time, Nora spoke about her father and her mother, who at the time were in the hostile throes of separation. She was tormented by the thought of her parents the way one can only be at twenty-five, when you suddenly realize that while you prefer to be an adult who is not like them, you may not succeed at it.

The night we were wearing the wigs, I made her laugh by imitating the Russian guy, Alexei, with whom I shared an office on the ground floor. For a month he'd been living in the room where we worked, to save on rent. He'd equipped it with an electric burner on which he heated the nasty contents of various canned food products, and at night he laid a sleeping bag on top of our joined desks, evading the guards. He put everything away before I arrived, except when he didn't hear the alarm go off. Unexpectedly, Nora kissed me. Since we were wearing wigs and I was imitating the broken English of a Russian, in a sense we were and weren't ourselves, but maybe that's always the way it is when you kiss someone new on the lips.

I tell all this to Mrs. A. as we wait, to distract her more than anything else, but she must already know the story, or isn't too interested, because when a young woman appears with a head-shaped wooden stand on which her new hair is resting, she leaps to her feet.

The fake hair is remarkably similar in color and style to hers, but I'd be willing to bet that the texture is quite different. Mrs. A. sits down in front of a mirror and lets the girl place it on her head ceremoniously, like a crown. She stares raptly at her reflection, turning to one side and the other, and asks the young woman for a handheld mirror to check the back.

"I look almost better with than without it," she says, and I can't decide if it's to cheer herself up or if she really thinks that. With that synthetic hair, she is certainly different from before: different yet also the same.

We are briefed on how to care for the wig: it can be combed and also washed with a mild shampoo, but not often; there's no need to, the wig's hair does not get dirty the way ours does (the young woman has the linguistic prudence to say "ours" instead of "real"). "And now you can choose a nightcap. It's complimentary, and we have them in different colors. Mint green, do you like this one? What do you think? It goes well with your eyes, too. Here, wait, I'll help you take it off."

Mrs. A. holds on to the wig with both hands. "No! I want to keep it on. If I can. So I can get used to it at least."

The young woman can't keep a sad expression from crossing her face. "Oh. Of course you can. It's yours now."

We leave the shop arm in arm. Mrs. A. is wearing her new hair, looking proud. "Let's not say anything to Nora. Let's see if she notices," she suggests. I promise to go along — it sounds like fun. Meantime I text a message to my wife, explaining that Babette will be wearing the wig and that she should pretend not to notice.

In the frenzy we forgot to take the wooden dummy. I go back to retrieve it a few days later, by myself. I tell the same girl, "Excuse me, but the lady lost her head." She, however, does not smile; perhaps the joke is in bad taste.

I leave the dummy in the car, on the passenger seat, until the next time I see Mrs. A. I even exchange a few words with it. One afternoon I offer a young colleague a ride home. As he gets into the car, he looks up, puzzled. "And just what are you doing with this?" he asks. Then, giving me no time to explain, he bows to kiss her lipless face.

THE HALL OF MEMORABILIA

Mrs. A. does not lose her hair during the first cycle of chemotherapy, nor during the second either. Instead she vomits continually, which is perhaps worse. She's placed three basins in strategic locations — beside the couch, under the bed and in the bathroom — and is not reluctant to talk about how she uses them regularly. Reticence about bodily functions has never been part of her nature. She's a woman who goes straight to the point: one of those people — as she would describe herself — who choose to tell it like it is. What she can't stand is having everyone in town ask her how she is. Who cares? She's lost thirteen pounds in a little over a month, she is visibly emaciated, so she's not too surprised that everyone asks about her health. To avoid it she goes out as seldom as possible and now prefers to do her shopping at the market in Almese, a few miles farther away; in any case, it's on her way back from the hospital.

The doctors have advised against raw vegetables, preserves packed in oil and sausages — everything with a potential bacterial content that might threaten her weakened immune system, a kind of pregnant-woman's diet that she has not experienced in better circumstances. And just like a pregnant woman, in the brief periods when she is unaffected by the treatment and its aftereffects, she indulges in sporadic yearnings for particular foods, which she perhaps ironically calls "my cravings."

One day she gets into the car and drives for miles and miles, only because she's recalled the bread baked in a wood-burning oven in Giaveno. She's spent a lifetime denying herself such whims in the name of exemplary conduct, out of respect for . . . respect for what? She'd had a yen for that bread many times before but had never ventured to go and get it because it seemed inconvenient to face that winding road just to satisfy an impulse. Now she clings to her desires, she invokes them, because each one corresponds to a burst of vitality that for a few minutes distracts her from the overwhelming thought of the illness.

Parmigiano cheese is the first to vanish from her refrigerator, followed by cheeses in general, then red and white meats. The nausea isn't to blame for the meat, she explains; it's that she can no longer taste or smell it, and chewing a piece of meat without tasting it is like having something dead in your mouth, aware the whole time that it's dead: in the end it's impossible to swallow it.

"Last night I felt like peas and eggs. I cooked them and ate them eagerly. Then I started coughing and threw it all up. That's it, no more eggs and peas either."

Mrs. A., who never turned her nose up at even the most dubious traditional dishes — roasted frogs' legs, boiled snails, pigeon or tripe, fried brains and entrails — is now unable to consume an innocent plate of eggs and peas. "Water, too, can you believe it? Even that nauseates me." Starting in December, and for the entire year of life left to her, she will drink only carbonated beverages — Coke, aranciata and chinotto — and will eat mainly sweets, like an immoderate, incorrigible little girl.

I decide to go and see her. Informed of her absurd diet, I bring her a tray of small Baci di Dama cookies (observing their success, I show up with an identical tray at every future visit, until the end, until she refuses those, too). One sunny Sunday morning, I set out with Emanuele, who, to honor his defector-nanny has brought along an intensely colorful, almost psychedelic drawing, in which winged nymphs with pink, purple and blue hair float in a monster-infested sky.

"What are these?" I ask him.

"Delicate fairies."

"And those?"

"Pokémon."

"Oh."

Too bad he then decides to wrap the drawing: he balls it up like a candy and loads it with Scotch tape. What he hands to Mrs. A. is a gob of crumpled, sticky paper. She sets it aside, puzzled. She no longer has time to pursue Emanuele's creative excursions; she has her body to look after now, all those medicines to take and their side effects to be weighed against their benefits. I have the distinct feeling that the drawing will end up in the trash as soon as we leave.

Emanuele can't understand the self-centeredness the illness has forced on her. He can't conceive of Mrs. A. as a different person from the woman who took care of him, him and him alone, who followed him along his rambling fantasies wherever they were headed and spoiled him like a little prince. When he notices her unexpected remoteness, he becomes nervous and petulant. I can tell by the way his voice changes: he does that whenever he wants to be the center of attention. But Mrs. A. doesn't have the strength or the desire to understand what's going through the child's head. I find myself between two raging flames burning with expectations and resentment: on the one hand a sick elderly woman, on the other a schoolboy, each eager to have all eyes on him for fear of disappearing.

I send Emanuele out to play in the courtyard, even though it's cold. He protests but in the end obeys. From the doorway he gives me one of his most withering looks.

There was a room in Mrs. A.'s house where the radiators had been turned off for years, a room that looked not like either a living room or a study but rather a reliquary. Since in winter the temperature here was at least ten degrees lower than in the rest of the apartment, when you went in, you had the feeling you were entering a catacomb. The windows were shuttered with colored-glass panes depicting women's faces in profile — I don't recall the name of the stained-glass artist, but Mrs. A. always mentioned him very reverently — so the light that filtered through was also hushed, sepulchral. Everything in that room spoke of Renato.

A recessed wall had been fitted with shelves, and a different collection was displayed on each shelf. The mix of periods and styles suggested that the collector was an individual suffering from a peculiar incoherence or someone who was very open-minded: there were a dozen pre-Columbian statues, some bizarrely shaped paperweights that I had never seen anywhere else, painted ceramic sculptures of dubious taste, plus assorted silver and brass containers. In the center of the room, a low table with a false bottom displayed twenty or so pocketwatches, arranged equidistantly from one another on a green felt lining, the hands of each stopped at twelve noon. The aspiration of a secondhand dealer like Renato to become an art expert — a goal he came close to but never actually achieved — was evident from the heterogeneous nature of the collection. Whether Mrs. A. was aware of it is impossible to say, but she would not have dishonored her husband's dubious talent for anything in the world. Of all the experiences in her life, assisting him in his business dealings was certainly the most unexpected and exciting; just the thought of it still filled her with pride.

The most valuable objects were stacked behind a lacquered screen

with Oriental motifs: about fifty
canvases, all authenticated. I know
for a fact that there were works by
Aligi Sassu and Romano Gazzera,
at least a couple from the school of
Felice Casorati and some from the
futurist period, though not by its
most celebrated exponents. Mrs. A.
also spoke to me about an oil by
Giuseppe Migneco, *Gli sposi* (*The
Married Couple*), which Renato had
never wanted to sell, despite the
insistence of a doctor who in-
creased his offer each year. That
painting, she said, made her think
of her and Renato, and of me and
Nora.

Actually I've never seen even one
of the paintings. Mrs. A. let me see
only the paper packaging, all iden-

tical, and the one time I dared peek between the edges of a wrapper, she stepped forward to stop me. I didn't try it again.

"What are you planning to do with them?" I ask her on the day of the visit with Emanuele. It's an indelicate question that I have not considered properly, yet I feel it's my duty to warn her about the dissolution of her cherished collection that she has watched over for so long in an apartment that no one would ever suspect housed such treasure. Whoever comes later will not have the slightest regard for it, certainly not what she would expect, because there is no possible comparison with a devotion that's lasted a lifetime. Mrs. A. still has the luxury of preparing for her death — and to determine the fate of each of those objects exactly as she wishes.

"They're fine here," she replies.

The question creates a momentary rift: I realize it when she quickly invites me to leave that hall of memorabilia and move to the living room; she feels cold, she says. I know what she's thinking, and I can't blame her. Although I don't think I had an ulterior motive, still, I must admit that I noticed the painting of the nude woman about to peel peaches, and for a moment I imagined it hanging in Nora's and my bedroom, something that might seem intimate enough to be up there watching us every night, awake or asleep.

After that Sunday I found myself
in Mrs. A.'s apartment one more
time. She had been dead for four
months. In the end she'd left us
two matching pieces of furniture, a
table and a credenza from the twen-
ties, both cream-colored; I had to
hurry and pick them up before the
place was sold. Two pieces of furniture: Babette's only gift to us and
all we have left of her. She had not
provided for Emanuele.

Both cousins, Virna and Marcella,
were waiting for me. The table and
the credenza were the only furnishings remaining, along with a series
of cartons containing odds and
ends: a pressure cooker, two plastic

pitchers and a set of gold-rimmed glasses.

"Those we'll give to charity," Virna said.

"A noble intention," I remarked, without a hint of sarcasm.

Not a trace of the chandeliers, the collection of pocketwatches and the pre-Columbian statues, no sign of the paintings and the grandfather clock in the living room. Even the double panes of the windows were gone. Now the light of day invaded the room aggressively, as it had never been allowed to do before. It's an apartment that has been plundered, the swift demobilization of an entire lifetime devoted to preservation. Mrs. A. had had plenty of time, months and months, to ensure that those sacred objects be handed down and given some meaning, and she hadn't done anything. After the diagnosis she had focused on nothing but striving desperately each day to gain a few more futile hours for herself. There was not a sign left of her, or of all that she had watched over for a lifetime.

Poor, foolish Mrs. A.! You let yourself be duped — death tricked you, and the illness before that. Where are the paintings that you kept hidden behind the screen? For years you didn't even look at them, afraid the dust would damage them. Even the screen has disappeared, probably abandoned in some damp storeroom, wrapped in plastic and raised off the ground by a pallet. We have to consider the future, Mrs. A., always. You often boasted about how smart you were, how you learned everything you knew from experience, but unfortunately it didn't turn out to be very useful. You would have been better off thinking about it more, because your common sense wasn't enough to save you or your possessions. The end does not pardon us even the slightest of faults, even the most innocent of failings.

We placed the table in the kitchen. Emanuele recognized it and walked around it, not touching it, as if wondering what spatiotemporal channel had transported it from

Mrs. A.'s house, from the past, to here. The first night eating at it was strange; none of us was used to the chill of the marble surface, to its smooth feel as our forearms rested on it. The artificial light glared off the white tabletop into our eyes; the whole room was suddenly more brilliant.

"I'll have to get a lower-watt bulb," I said.

"Right," Nora replied, preoccupied. Then she added, "Don't you feel like we're eating with her?"

There was no room for the credenza: too wide, too bulky for our urban kitchen. We put it in the basement, to await a new spot that it is unlikely to be assigned. One morning when I went down to clean it and apply a product to protect it from termites, I noticed some fine wood particles piled up in the corners. Opening the upper doors, I saw that the interior walls were papered with various newspaper articles, each with a date written on it in ballpoint: 1975 or 1976. Those were years when Renato was still alive but already gravely incapacitated. As far as I know, the credenza had come to Mrs. A. from an aunt of his, perhaps on the occasion of their wedding.

I scanned the headlines of the clippings, trying to find a selection criterion that seemed to make sense to me:

DEATH PLOT, POLICE OFFICER AR-
RESTED

PENTAGON AND CIA CAUSED
DROUGHT IN CUBA?

ITT CONFIRMS IT FINANCED ANTI-
ALLENDE COUP

PUBLIC HOUSING TO BE HEATED BY
SOLAR ENERGY

BILLION-DOLLAR SALARY FOR COS-
METICS PRESIDENT

SAN GIORIO: FOUL-SMELLING LAND-
FILL

SHE, 50, HE, 67: "IT WAS LOVE AT
FIRST SIGHT"

At first glance the articles, about forty in all, did not show any logical connection. The only obvious feature was that they were not chosen by Mrs. A. (I doubt she had a clear idea of where Cuba is or that she knew the Pentagon as anything other than a five-sided geometrical figure.) Nevertheless, looking from side to side, from one clipping to the next, I began to see that the articles conveyed several basic themes. I counted, grouping them by subject. Surprisingly, in the final count the majority involved the CIA, the FBI and the troubled relations between the United States and Fidel Castro. Mrs. A. had never mentioned any particular interest Renato might have had in the intrigues of power, not even during our last conversations. The inside of the credenza, however, introduced me to a man fascinated by conspiracy, who by pasting those clippings side by side was perhaps trying to extrapolate an overall picture that might reveal the ruse into which society had drawn him. Maybe it was even more than that: perhaps Renato collaborated with the secret services — Mrs. A. never failed to describe him as an unpredictable man, someone with many lives and therefore extremely interesting — though it is unlikely that an intelligence agent would have pasted articles about the CIA in the kitchen credenza.

A box circled with a marking pen recorded a list of the ten most powerful companies in the world, according to '73 data. Chrysler was in fifth place. If Renato only knew what's happened in the meantime — how Chrysler went up in smoke and is now under the leadership of one of his fellow countrymen — he'd think the planet had reversed its rotation around its axis.

If Nora's and my furniture were to end up at auction one day, or if it were to be found under the ashes of a volcanic eruption, it would hold almost no sign of us, just some furtive scribblings by Emanuele, like cave paintings, dating from the period when every corner of the house was threatened by his markers. The archaeologists of the future would not find any photographs; the few we have reside on the computer's hard disk, which will have already been useless for many years. We have a strange iconoclastic mania, Nora and I: we don't save anything, we don't exchange letters or notes (with the exception of grocery lists), we don't buy souvenirs when traveling because for the most part they are tacky and the same items can now be found throughout the world; also, since thieves visited the apartment, we don't keep gold or jewelry — we simply don't own any. The testimony of our lives together is dependent upon a good memory, ours and that of a silicon motherboard. No, Nora, the two of us don't consider the future either. We don't have a wedding album, can you imagine? Yet one day we'll find ourselves far enough away from that day that we'll want to relive it, at least in pictures.

The archaeologists who will come and blow away the ashes from our house will unearth only the metal parts of the sophisticated furnishings, and it will take them some time to reconstruct their original beauty; they will find very few objects and almost no embellishments, not even in Emanuele's room, which from year to year is being emptied of toys and colors, because everything that's important to him is now found in the circuits of a tablet. I wonder what would suggest to them that a couple and then a family had lived in those rooms and that they were happy together, at least for long stretches of time.

And if through some complicated process of fossilization a few scraps of newspaper were to survive among the papers accumulated in the wastebasket and not yet discarded, then, scanning the headlines as I had with the articles in Mrs. A.'s credenza, they might perhaps think of a second Dark Age, the passage of another dismal, unpromising millennium. Or maybe we're only impressionable. We view our era as grim and endangered, just as Renato's seemed grim and endangered to him. Every age contains within itself the arrogant claim of catastrophe.

BEIRUT

"Without her I don't feel up to it," Nora confesses as the first Christmas without Babette approaches. Mrs. A. has decided not to spend Christmas Eve with us but rather with her cousins. She always described them as envious and spiteful and kept away from them even though she was alone, but the cancer seems to have weakened her immune system against her family as well, defenses that she'd spent half a lifetime building up. Or

143

maybe she didn't expect us to invite her again this year. Maybe she'd said to herself, Now that I'm no longer their housekeeper, there's no reason they should want me. When I called to tell her she would be welcome as always, she seemed bewildered, almost annoyed. "Oh, please, I can't even think about sitting down at the table. Seeing all that food. By now I'm too difficult for company."

I suggested she join us before or after dinner, whether she ate or not — we would be happy to see her just the same.

"Forget about me," she cut me off. "Enjoy your holiday and don't worry."

Nora and I aren't at all unworried, however. Without Mrs. A. the list of those invited to Christmas Eve dinner looms more threatening than ever: the three of us, Nora's mother, her second husband, Antonio — a passionate commentator on the economic crisis and an inflammatory, overaged blogger — and his daughter, Marlene, with whom Nora has never bonded, perhaps because of the ten-year age difference or because, as she bitterly maintains, it is wholly unnatural to love a parent's new child, to form attachments on demand. With Christmas the separation of Nora's parents intensifies like a storm cloud, and she allows herself to be charged by the electrostatic potential in the air, constantly on the verge of discharging ten thousand volts on anyone who comes within range, in this case Emanuele or me. Not disappointing anyone — my family members, hers and their acquired relations — while at the same time avoiding awkward run-ins — is a game of skill that we can never seem to master.

At least with Mrs. A., an element of stability had been assured. When the serious lack of common topics became evident at the table, along with an equally serious lack of desire to find some, we focused our attention on the dishes she had prepared for us. We praised them, proposed suggestions for the following year, and in that way we dragged on until midnight. Mrs. A. became the center of Christmas, or its victim, but either way she was flattered. On that evening, more than on any other occasion, she seemed like one of the family, even if she really couldn't bring herself to remain seated in the place we'd assigned her. Moving frenziedly between the dining room and the kitchen, leaving conversations midway, she would start washing the dishes earlier than necessary, changing her role every five minutes: from waitress to guest, then back to waitress. In retrospect it must have been nerve-racking for her. When it came time for dessert, I took the situation in hand and forced her to stay put. "Now, keep your behind glued to that chair," and she liked the fact that I spoke to her so firmly. She clasped her hands in her lap and enjoyed the evening's epilogue.

She had no gifts for anyone, but there were always a couple for her, from us and from Nora's mother. In truth the one from Nora's mother was pretty paltry — I suspect that it had been recycled more than once. Their relationship had never been entirely accepting. After all, Nora often indelicately revealed her deep fondness for Babette.

There always came a time at the Christmas dinner during which a merciless comparison was made between the roasts, the one prepared by my mother-in-law versus the one made by Mrs. A. The two pans were placed on the table, side by side. The dueling women exchanged a long look, like in a female western. Already stuffed, we all obediently took a bite from each slice in turn, then went on with our praises, more emphatic and more clamorous than before. Despite the fact that we tried to weigh them equally, in the end Mrs. A.'s scored more points, as always.

"We'll escape. That's what we'll do," Nora suggests. We take advantage of an offer on a Beirut flight departing on December 24. We counter her mother's protests by saying that the flights were cheaper, much cheaper, knowing that economic considerations have the power to silence her (the vicissitudes of the divorce have compellingly elevated money to the top of her scale of values). As for Emanuele, we assure him that he will receive his gifts just the same — earlier, in fact — and he seems pacified as well.

It's odd the way certain customs are established: Mrs. A.'s cancer and her untimely demise led Nora and me to make a secret, forbidden pact. Never again would we celebrate Christmas with our parents. From one December to the next, we would always save up enough money to take us far away during those days, away from family tempests and conventions whose value we now doubted.

On the plane I read a book by Siddhartha Mukherjee, *The Emperor of All Maladies.* After years of exploring the murky territory at the intersection between hematology and oncology, Mukherjee, an Indian American, wrote a fictionalized "biography" of cancer in six hundred pages, dense with references, and soon won a Pulitzer Prize. Each paragraph holds Mrs. A. up to the light and denies me one more milligram of hope for her. Mukherjee describes an all-out war, one marked by a few prominently featured successes but, in the end, a failed venture.

I pause over the analogy that the Greek physician Galen had drawn between cancer and melancholy, both brought on by an excess of black humor. As I read, it's as though I can feel the viscous liquid, a stream of tar, clogging my lymphatic system. My dear Mrs. A., according to ancient medicine, we are cut from the same cloth; we are paladins of the black.

I'd like to call my therapist to stem the anxiety that is rapidly taking hold of me, but it's impossible from here — use one of the pay phones in the plane's cabin? Do they really work? in any case it's Christmas Eve, and he wouldn't answer — so I ask the stewardess for another miniature bottle of French wine. She serves it scornfully after letting me wait for quite a while. She must be a Muslim, or possibly she just finds the spectacle of a father getting drunk while sitting beside his son disgraceful.

I suspect that the stewardess knows nothing about black humor, and for that matter neither does Nora, sweetly asleep against my shoulder. I watch her, not sure whether I'm moved or envious. Her lymph flows freely, limpid and copious in spite of everything. I am convinced that her vitality is inexhaustible, that nothing, not even the ultimate sorrow, not even the gravest loss, would be able to deter it. In the end we are almost never happy or unhappy because of what happens to us; we are one or the other depending on the humor that flows inside us, and hers is molten silver: the whitest of metals, the best conductor and the most merciless reflector. The consolation of knowing that she is so strong mixes with the fear of not being truly indispensable to her, with the suspicion that I might be sucking the life out of her, like a kind of gigantic parasite.

One night we were talking about Mrs. A. and her life marked by sacrifice. Right in the middle of it, just when her body was at its most vital, she had enjoyed five years of perfect happiness with her husband, before his kidneys faltered. Five years that had left no visible traces except in her, five years of marriage plus one of engagement

during which she had distanced
herself from who she'd been before
and accumulated enough memories
to endure the sight of Renato dying before her eyes, day after day,
inexorably, in hundreds of dialysis
sessions that changed his blood and
his disposition and his love for her.
Five years that had been enough
for her to get by for another forty
of them.

"Could you do it?" Nora had
asked me. "Would you be able to
stand it? Would you have the forti-
tude to stay with me until the end
if I got sick?"

"We both swore to it, if I remember correctly."

"What if the illness lasted as long
as Renato's? Would you stay with

me all that time, wasting the best years of your life?"

"Yes, I would."

I knew I shouldn't turn the question around, because people whose lymph flows freely are as unstoppable as a rushing stream. But there are some conversations between people in love that, once you cross a certain threshold, inevitably draw you into their dark center.

"And you?"

Nora's right hand went to the lock of hair that curls behind her ear, a strand that remains hidden except when she gathers her hair back, and that my fingers always go searching for. She started twisting and tugging it. "I don't know. I think so," but for a moment she had hesitated. For the rest of the evening, we kept away from each other.

On the plane headed for the temperate latitudes of the Middle East, a few hours after midnight on Christmas Eve, with my family asleep and nothing out there to threaten us at the moment, I feel like I am at a high point in our lives. I wonder how long it will last and how best to savor it fully. Certainly not by trying to dull my senses with more wine, which I didn't even want. Then, too, Nora and I are always so busy, so distracted, so tired. We live in anticipation, constantly waiting for something that will free us from the burdens of the present, without taking into account new ones that will arise. If these really are our best years, I'm not satisfied with how we're using them. I'd like to wake her up and tell her that, but I know she wouldn't take me seriously; she would turn around in her seat, snuggle up even more, lean her head against the darkened window and go on sleeping.

THE SEVEN-TIMES TABLE

Among the articles pasted inside
Mrs. A.'s credenza were a few that
had particularly intrigued me: An
American, Terry Feil, had died
thirty years after absorbing radiation in Nagasaki, where he landed
soon after the explosion of the
bomb. In Britain, in the seventies,
fifty thousand people a year died
owing to pulmonary and cardiovas-
cular disease, the theory being —
according to the article — that the
consumption of nicotine had some-

thing to do with the deaths. In Italy a harmful drug had remained on the market for more than five years. Ionizing radiation, pulmonary carcinomas, drugs — it was as if the shadow of death, which at that time had already darkened Renato's field of vision to some extent, were advancing toward Mrs. A. and her husband was aware of it. Looking at the newspaper clippings he'd so meticulously preserved, I wondered if he'd had a premonition about his wife's end. Perhaps he feared it more than his own — and in those seemingly disconnected accounts he had been searching for a way to save her.

Instead, thirty-five years later, Mrs. A. is offering her left arm to a needle that contains an alarming concentration of unstable isotopes of fluorine. She has always had thin, fragile blood vessels, making injections torture, but today she is full of optimism and isn't bothered by the nurse's clumsy attempts. If she goes by how she's been feeling for a couple of weeks — energetic and spirited, with smooth skin and a bit of appetite that has quickly allowed her to regain more than four pounds — she can't help but be convinced that she's cured or has at least embarked on the road to rapid improvement. The PET scan will confirm it for sure. The thought never crosses her mind that the upturn is entirely due to the abnormal doses of cortisone she's been taking for months; the doubt doesn't arise even when, at the end of the scan, she meets the uncomfortable gaze of the technician who, from inside the protective lead-walled cubicle, has seen her diaphanous body displayed on the monitor, the ghost of a woman who has lit up in several areas besides the lung: the L1 vertebra, the ileum and the right femoral neck. The cancerous cells have emitted packets of positrons that in annihilation with their negative twins have been converted into light, a clear sign that the cancer has now entered the bloodstream and is taking full possession of the body.

But Mrs. A. doesn't know it yet, and for the moment she's relieved, a relief motivated also by something beyond her physical well-being and of which she feels somewhat ashamed. A week ago the painter died, quietly, in his sleep. That evening he ate and drank heartily, and in the morning he did not wake up. What this means, in addition to the inexorable shortening of the list of people with whom she's shared the past, is that the bird of paradise had not come for her: they'd both been wrong about that. It's good news, no use pretending otherwise, and in any case the painter had nothing to complain about. "For a midget he went far beyond what could be expected," is Mrs. A.'s cursory summation, "and he enjoyed it, all that glory and those women. He enjoyed every minute of it!"

I think that at the time of the PET scan, before being informed of its disastrous verdict, Nora may have shared Mrs. A.'s unfounded optimism; she may even have encouraged it in some way. When I asked her, though, she denied it, saying that in any case the idea of acupuncture hadn't been hers but her mother's.

"Acupuncture? Did you seriously take her to have acupuncture? When exactly?"

"Before the report came."

"She had an advanced-stage cancer, and you two . . . I can't believe it."

Nora's tardy confession came one night when we had a couple of friends over for dinner: not very close friends, a daughter the same age as Emanuele, a similar lifestyle and an acceptable geographical proximity. It happens more often than we'd like that certain omissions between us emerge while we are in the company of others, as if we wanted to make sure we had witnesses or accomplices — or, even more cowardly, as if we were trying to mitigate the other's possible reactions by having an outsider present.

Nora went on the defensive. "If it's as ineffective as you say, then it makes no difference."

Her reasoning was impeccable,

yet I felt there was something wrong with it — that falling into the trap of superstition, convincing herself that there was an easy remedy, was the ultimate trick the cancer had played on Mrs. A. Her sixteen-month ordeal still wasn't enough for me to decide whether the biggest favor we could do her was to make her face the truth or, conversely, to foster a false hope, but I was certainly leaning more toward blunt realism.

"Which would you prefer?" I asked our guests. "Given such a diagnosis, I mean. Wouldn't you at least like to have the honor of not being taken for a fool?"

They both hedged. They sensed that I was more involved than I let on, and perhaps the cancer of a person close to someone didn't seem like a topic to engage in over dessert.

"My lucidity is more important to me than anything else," I said. "I wouldn't like to betray it at the very end."

"How sad," Nora remarked, implying that not only was I embarrassing our friends but that I had just offended her.

"Why do you say that?"

She picked up the empty bowls abruptly. "Drop it. You wouldn't understand."

When we were alone, I tried to coax her to forgive me by making her laugh. I reminded her of how she had insisted that we consult a vegan pediatrician, years ago, for Emanuele. "Remember? He wanted us to wean the baby on caraway and millet seeds, like a chicken." And about the time she'd sent me to a renowned hypnotist in the city to treat my insomnia. (Both her mother's suggestions.) At the hypnotist's I had not lapsed into a state of trance — in fact, I was more alert than ever the whole time. "What do you see?" the doctor kept asking me in a baritone voice.

"Nothing, sorry."

I sensed his irritability growing, and I in turn got worked up because I felt like I was disrespecting him. At one point during the relaxation exercise, my head had started spinning sharply. He quickly latched onto that symptom, interpreting the dizziness as the residual effect of a cochlear disorder. "I bet you had the mumps."

"You're right. When I was five, though."

"Aha, there you are. You were scared, weren't you?"

"I don't know."

"Of course you were scared! Think about that helpless child experiencing a dizzy spell for the first time. He has no idea what is happening to him, and he is afraid, so afraid. Do you see him?"

"I . . ."

"Pick him up."

"Pick him up? Who?"

"Take that child in your arms.

Cradle him gently, caress him. Take care of the child you were, whisper to him not to be afraid. . . ."

One, two, three! — and, satisfied, he woke me up.

"All those things I always mistook for atrocious traumas could be the result of mumps," I said to my wife, who was finally smiling. "See what you led me to discover, you and that visionary mother of yours? Come over here, a little closer, help me cradle the suffering child in me."

The fact is that Nora, her mother and Mrs. A. had indeed gone to the acupuncturist; all three together went to the blind doctor who had enabled my mother-in-law to quit smoking and then to quit gorging herself on ice cream in the middle of the night, who had relieved her low-back pain, the migraines that had become excruciating after the divorce, an episode of hemorrhoids and some general problems of self-esteem.

"How can an acupuncturist be blind?" I took the liberty of asking her one day.

"He became blind as a result of diabetes. Sometimes he forgets to remove a needle, but you realize it when you take a shower."

At the very least, on that occasion Mrs. A. had undressed in front of someone who couldn't attest to her sad decline. The doctor sought the points in which to insert the needles by probing her skin with warm, sensitive fingertips. Mrs. A. was shaking (partly because of the cold); he noticed it and placed his palms over her ears for a few seconds, whereupon the shivering ceased instantly. How long had it been since a man touched her so gently? The doctors always protected themselves with gloves, and they were almost all young and glacial, but the acupuncturist with the unseeing eyes . . . he had a delicate touch and a lovely voice, mellow and deep.

He'd explained to her how the whorls of the auricle contain the form of an upside-down fetus, a fetus waiting to see the light, and how by opportunely stimulating the nerve centers of that miniature individual it is possible to heal the body in its entirety. Mrs. A. listened intently, eating up his words and picturing the diminutive copy of the tumor inside her ear; she imagined it pierced by the needle. At the same instant, by magic, the one in her chest dissolved as well.

"Will it hurt?" she asked.

"Not at all. The needles are very fine."

"Too bad."

She wanted the monster in her to die painfully, for it to experience what she'd been going through, at least for a moment. The ambivalence that she exhibited toward the cancer at that stage was curious: on some occasions she spoke of it as a trampled part of herself, on others as an alien life trapped inside her body, to be eradicated, period.

"Now close your eyes," the blind doctor had said, "and think of something pleasurable."

Something pleasurable. And so, for the first time in a long while, as she lay on yet another bed in yet another doctor's office, motionless so that the needles sticking out of her body like a porcupine's wouldn't bend or move or penetrate more deeply, Mrs. A. recalled the day in late October when Renato had married her, the maple trees with their bloodred leaves like wounds on the valley's slopes. She'd worn a dress that a seamstress had sewn, identical to that of

Paola Ruffo of Calabria, but to make it more personal she had ordered a coronet of white rosebuds from a milliner on Via XX Settembre. Everything must still be in the armoire, the dress and the coronet's frame, along with her wedding trousseau, which she had quickly stored away and then never dared take out again. She was stung by sharp regret thinking about the sheets and tablecloths, so costly and never used due to excessive regard.

Then, through some train of association, maybe because he was in the habit of opening all the closet doors in the house to see what was inside, Mrs. A.'s attention shifted to Emanuele. She recalled the morning when he decided to let go of the chair leg, take three uncertain steps toward her and finally cling to her stockings. It had been Mrs. A. who'd witnessed that miracle. Nora and I were slightly affronted, in part because she had not stopped crowing about it. "He started to walk with me," she would proclaim proudly, and then she'd start to describe the scene all over again. Emanuele heard her repeat it so many times that he ended up mistaking that story for a memory. "Yes, I'm sure. I let go of the chair and toddled over to her. I clung to her stockings." Since Babette passed away, we've given up contradicting him.

■ ■ ■ ■

There was something that Mrs. A. often said about our son: "Just try to measure him up against ten other boys his age. Compared to him they all seem like monkeys." To some extent she was not mistaken. From the time he was born, Emanuele's body had been well proportioned and harmonious, his features flawless, the difference between him and his peers already visible when he was in the ward, surrounded by the other plastic cradles. In the hospital room, Nora and Mrs. A. exclaimed over the perfect shape of his head, so small and round — the C-section had favored that — and his skin, clear and smooth from the beginning, none of the redness that made other newborns look blotchy.

A few weeks later, I, too, who considered myself immune to the wonder, had fallen under the spell of his beauty. I kept him glued to me as long as I could, until he was four or five years old. Sometimes a shameful thing happened to me: holding my son's soft, naked body close stirred uncontrollable signs of sexual arousal. They were physical responses unrelated to any thought, but all the same they left me appalled, and for that reason I pulled away more than once. When Nora noticed it, she caressed me first and then him. "There's nothing wrong with it," she said. "I, too, can feel him with all my organs."

Then Emanuele grew up, more quickly than we thought, and we found ourselves wanting him to grow up fast, not realizing that we would soon miss him as a little child. He was never quick enough, he was never responsible enough, his reasoning was never sufficiently thought out. Only with Mrs. A. did he allow himself to regress to the condition of the small child he still felt he was. She held him in her arms, rocking him for hours; she let him be capricious and repetitive in his expressions, and she attended to those things that we thought he should already be doing on his own. (Yet didn't Nora and I behave the same way with her, abandoning ourselves to her care?) Maybe it was her hovering presence that prevented me from seeing Emanuele as he really was: not a prodigy but an average, if not slightly below-average child, one inclined to be touchy, for whom grasping something, especially something abstract, always involved effort, anxiety and the need for exhausting repetition. Realizing that was as painful for us as it was for him, and, perhaps unfairly, I find myself blaming Mrs. A., since for a long time she was his shield.

I remember an incident. In kindergarten Emanuele had not shown any aptitude for drawing; his doodles had something alarming about them, but we didn't pay too much attention (how important is it in life to know how to color within the lines?), at least not until the afternoon when I went to pick him up at school and I noticed the children's self-portraits in tempera paint, arranged next to one another to form a border. Emanuele's was different from the others: a shapeless pink blob with two black slanting strokes to indicate the eyes. Conscious of the difference, he felt compelled to quickly set the record straight. "Mine is the ugliest," he said, as if there were any need to state it.

Later I told Nora and Mrs. A. about it. It was a sheer outpouring of disappointment: if our son was further behind than the others in drawing, that was a clear sign that he would be behind in a host of other things — I drew very well at his age — and we would have to deal with it. Being a parent, it seemed to me, also involved being constantly exposed to the possibility of humiliation.

Nora and Mrs. A. listened to me with their arms crossed. Then, not saying a word, without my having the slightest idea of their intentions or any way to stop them, they left the house and marched straight to Emanuele's school. There, acting together just like a mother and daughter, they insisted on the immediate removal of the tempera paintings. Then they returned home victorious, their outrage still not having simmered down.

Nevertheless, going forward, our son's comparison with his peers became increasingly apparent, and their countermeasures were no longer enough. By the beginning of second grade, Emanuele continued to confuse *b* and *d,* right and left, before and after: to me it seemed unacceptable.

"It seems unacceptable to you because your concept of intelligence is limited," Nora retorted. "He has a great imagination. But for you and your family, that doesn't count, right? For you people, scholastic perfection is the only thing that matters."

"What does my family have to do with it now?"

"Two anthropologists and their young physicist, with the most brilliant academic grades and journal publications. Tell the truth, why don't you admit that having a son who is not a mathematical genius makes you feel diminished?"

Oh, was she ever right. But that time my answer was deliberately spiteful. "Unfortunately, a bent for mathematics is genetic."

She shook her head. "And he was unlucky enough to inherit it from the wrong side, I suppose?"

Now here we are, Emanuele and me, facing each other on yet another Saturday morning, the moment we both hate most in the entire week. We're sitting at the dining-room table, a table of raw beechwood that Nora commissioned from one of her designers in Belgium and has now made us terrified of using, for fear of leaving ballpoint marks on it. Slowly I leaf through the arithmetic notebook, the smell of the glossy plastic cover taking me back to an identical one from my childhood. It looks like a battlefield: there are red marks everywhere, diagonal lines crossing out entire pages, objections and exclamation points.

"What happened here?" I ask.

"The teacher tore out the sheet."

"Why?"

"I got it all wrong."

We struggle for half an hour with the multiplication tables, both of us more and more sullen.

"Seven times one?"

"Seven."

"Seven times six?"

Emanuele counts on his fingers, painfully slow. "Forty-four."

"No, forty-two. Seven times zero?"

"Seven."

It's ironic, or rather no, it's atrocious: with a degree in theoretical physics, a major in quantum field theory and a general familiarity with the most advanced formalism of calculus, I am unable to transfer into my son's head an understanding of why any number times zero results in zero. I seem to see the inside of his skull, the brain floating in a foggy mist where assertions dissolve without constructing any meaning.

I lose my patience. "It's zero! Zero! If you can't grasp it, then just get used to it!"

Forming an empty circle with my thumb and index finger, I hold it up two inches from his nose; it's clear that with that zero I'm describing him.

"But it's not in the multiplication table," he defends himself.

"The multiplication table has nothing to do with it! It's that you're dense!"

At that point Nora intervenes and asks me to leave; she'll continue with him. From the kitchen, where I try to regain my composure, I

hear her doing the multiplications
for him.

WINTER

Sometimes, after years of living together, you see signs no matter where you turn: traces of the person with whom you've shared a space for so long. I often come across Nora in every corner of our house, as if her spirit had settled on the objects like a fine dust, while Mrs. A., even during her last year, would encounter Renato's tenuous hologram everywhere she went. Whenever she paused at the window to look out at the steep driveway to the street, she remembered the day when, violating her husband's orders, she had stolen the keys from the tray in the entry hall and taken the car out of the garage. He didn't want her to drive, but he was sick and had to be brought to the hospital three times a week for dialysis, and who else could do it if she didn't?

"I scraped the right side against the corner," she told me, "and then I went home and told him, 'Prepare yourself!' "

She often mentioned that timid, heroic undertaking; she considered it an important step, simultaneously encompassing the beginning of Renato's decline and the dawn of her emancipation. Until then their union had been an orderly one, much more orderly than Nora's and mine. We were continually trading the roles of husband and wife to the point where we could no longer tell who was responsible for what. Renato drove, Mrs. A. didn't; Mrs. A. dusted the furniture, Renato didn't — each task had been assigned to only one of them from the beginning. A marriage lived outside the preestablished roles was foreign to her. It may be that this contributed to the security her presence gave us, because through her we experienced a somewhat shameful nostalgia for an outmoded, simplified model of the family, a model in which everyone does not have to be everything at once — male and female, logical and emotional, submissive and strict, romantic and prosaic — a model that differs from the one that in our time saddles us with such broad, undifferentiated responsibilities and makes us feel constantly inadequate no matter what.

For the most part, Mrs. A. was indulgent toward our domestic promiscuity, excusing it as a modern flaw, yet she instinctively opposed it. She couldn't stand to see me fumbling with the laundry, nor could she conceive of Nora taking a drill and boring a hole in a wall (a job at which my wife is actually much more skillful than I am). At those times she found a way to

shoo us out and do the task for us
— she who was indeed capable of
taking care of everything, since
widowhood had turned her into a
perfectly androgynous creature. In
a sense her death was also a chance
at salvation: had we relied on her
perspective for too long, we might
have found ourselves trapped in the
roles of the intrepid husband and
the submissive wife, in a rerun of
marriage as conceived fifty years
ago.

She was a conventional woman,
steeped in doctrine and inevitably
chauvinistic, but she didn't know
it. It's uncanny how her way of ad-
dressing me, slightly more deferen-
tial than the way she spoke to
Nora, confirmed me as the boss of

the house. She acted as if she had no choice but to give more credence to my opinions, more attention to my needs, more importance to my qualities than to those of my wife, despite the fact that her affection was all for Nora.

One summer I persuaded Nora to take an early vacation with her mother and Emanuele. During that brief period of bachelorhood, Mrs. A. looked after me with more care than ever before. She indulged herself in preparing dishes that Nora would have forbidden and often stayed to eat dinner in the evening — something she'd never done — in order to keep me company. In the morning she arrived earlier than usual, bearing the daily harvest from her vegetable garden. By the time I got up, she had already set the table for breakfast and placed a bag with my lunch next to my backpack: I would eat it later at the university instead of the cafeteria's sandwiches that, she said, would only weigh me down. She even brought a bunch of orange gerberas that she set in the center of the table. She played the role of the dutiful wife, and I did not stop her.

It was a muggy July, and we had not yet installed the air conditioners, so I walked around the apartment in my underwear. I had the impression that her eyes followed me, that she liked to look at me. As absurd as it may seem, after a week a faint erotic charge hovered in the rooms.

By the time Nora came back, I had grown used to that strange intimacy. The first time my wife saw me appear in my underwear in front of Mrs. A., she asked me to follow her into the bedroom, where she ordered me to put on some pants.

"So now you're even jealous of Babette?" I teased. "I don't think she has any particular designs on me, you know."

"She's still a woman," Nora said very seriously. "Don't forget that."

The window from which Renato watched Mrs. A. tackle the ramp with the car, his heart in his mouth, is the same one from which she, in February, looks out at a blank scene. A disturbance in the Atlantic has settled over the northern part of the peninsula and all told has dumped more snow than we've seen in the last ten years. Temperatures haven't risen above zero, not even in the middle of the day, and adamantine corridors of ice cover the streets, causing people to fracture wrists, ankles and sacra. Given the overcrowding in the emergency rooms, Civil Defense has recommended that everyone stay home, and Mrs. A. is among the few to obey.

None of the tenants has bothered to shovel the snow from the courtyard; rather than exert themselves, they prefer to park along the street. She was the only one who shoveled as long as she had the strength, as long as there was a good reason to go out, and that good reason was us. When it snowed, we tried to persuade her to stay over for the night — a folding cot was ready and waiting in Emanuele's room — but Mrs. A. wanted to go back to her own home, maybe because Renato's spirit awaited her for dinner, so she braved the slippery roads to Rubiana in her minuscule car. "She comes to us despite the storm," Nora would remark, surprised each time by such dedication. "My mother, on the other hand, won't drive if there's a trace of fog. When I was little, she wouldn't take me to the dentist because of the fog, so now all my teeth are in bad shape. What a witch."

Anyone outside who glimpsed Mrs. A.'s silhouette at the window would wonder if it was a man or a woman. Her gauntness has obliterated her feminine attributes: on her bald, seemingly shrunken head, she sports the mint green nightcap — during the third cycle of chemotherapy she suddenly lost all her hair — and by this time she routinely wears a dark sweater and slacks that are loose on her, like a prison uniform. That's exactly what she is: a prisoner. The soft layer of snow on the ground, a sight that has always enchanted her, now seems like an insuperable impediment.

Bad weather has kept her trapped in the apartment for fourteen consecutive days. Twice Giulietta's husband has done her shopping for her, a basic list very different from what she would have bought for herself. People who take care of us are almost never able to do things the way we'd like, but we have to make do: they've already done enough. A little clump of snow falls off the man's boots as he asks her the obvious questions, then melts on the floor of the entryway, going no further, a thin puddle that she doesn't bother to wipe up.

Her visits are limited to this. Her hermitage is difficult to reach.

Cancer, her worst enemy, is the only company still left to her. She no longer cares about anything except the clinical schedule that marks the days, weeks, months. By now she spends entire afternoons in bed, with the TV on, dozing in front of images of glowing girls talking about their numerous boy-friends — to her, a woman who has remained faithful to the same man all her life. Mrs. A. doesn't judge them harshly, she doesn't envy them. They simply belong to a new breed; they're extraterrestrials, and their adventures leave her indifferent.

The truth is that the PET scan and the second CT scan reveal a complete failure. The cancerous tumor has grown three millimeters in diameter, as if the toxins had scattered everywhere except where they were needed. The hair she'd sacrificed, the nearly thirty pounds she'd lost and the disgusting vomiting were all in vain. The oncologist who has been in charge of her case from the beginning doesn't show the slightest emotion as she pronounces all this; she never shows emotion, and it's an aspect of her character that Mrs. A. has come to appreciate, though earlier it seriously bothered her. The doctor has the Teutonic iciness of a military strategist, a coldness that goes well with her thick, wavy, auburn hair. She can't worry about the emotional fallout of every report she provides, or otherwise, with thirty patients hovering on the brink of survival or death, her frame of mind would be a constantly spinning centrifuge. "But there's a positive side," she added, "for the moment no other metastases have appeared. The tumor seems . . . frozen."

Nora was also present at the consultation, having insisted on accompanying Mrs. A.; maybe she had a presentiment that it would go badly. Later she would tell me how the doctor had chosen a metaphor in tune with the weather conditions to lie to Babette. While Mrs. A. was in the bathroom recomposing her tear-ravaged face,

Nora had asked, "How much time does she have?"

The doctor sighed, displaying a certain impatience with that kind of question, since sooner or later in cancer situations someone always came along wanting to know a date, to trivialize the sense of the treatment, and in this case it was Nora.

"Six months. Maybe."

In retrospect one might say that she was too harsh, that she had not taken into account Mrs. A.'s exceptional mettle: in the end she underestimated it by almost fifty percent.

On the fifteenth day of being shut in, Mrs. A. wakes up with a pain in her hand so acute that she starts screaming. She calls the medical responders. From behind their windows, the building's tenants watch the ambulance slipping and sliding dangerously on the ramp, its flashing lights tinting the blanket of snow blue and orange. Finally they see Mrs. A., wrapped up in an aluminum blanket, bundled into the rear door.

After that morning she will never again get into her sky blue Fiat Seicento. This was the end of her emancipation. All it took was one surrender to find out she no longer had the necessary courage; now the sole thought of driving a vehicle, even just a tricycle, of simultaneously managing the steering wheel, the pedals, the gearshift, of looking in the mirrors and keeping an eye on the host of other vehicles that pass her or come at her from the opposite direction, terrifies her, as if those actions, taken together, which until a moment ago had been interrelated, had now lost their cohesion. The car stays put for the rest of the winter, its battery discharging minute by minute, until a cousin — I don't know which one — goes to pick it up, to give it to a nephew or sell it.

Mrs. A. fills out the application forms to request transportation to and from the hospital. The immediate positive response she receives contains the words "permanent disability" and the adjective "critical," two terms she would complain about at length.

■ ■ ■ ■

It must have been more or less at that time that I spoke to my therapist about Mrs. A. As he listened to me, he jiggled his right leg impatiently and smoked more than usual. During one session he said something that at the moment sounded gratuitous and scornful: "All these cancer stories are the same."

We discussed whether it was reasonable to think that the circumstances of a person's death reflect in part what that person had been in life. Did Mrs. A. deserve what was happening to her, had she at any rate contributed to bringing it upon herself? Because what she could not seem to accept was first and foremost how unfair that punishment appeared.

I had a grandfather who had been a petty man, who didn't like anybody long before the onset of his dementia, so irascible that he instilled in me a profound animosity against the elderly and old age in general. For him, falling from a ladder propped against a cherry tree and lying there, dying, on the ground all night, unnoticed, as the rain drenched him, was indeed a fitting end. But Mrs. A., what sins did she have to atone for? And if it made sense to look for a correlation between the dynamics of death and the failures of life, then what end could I expect for myself?

The therapist, who is generally overcome with enthusiasm when it comes to analogies, interrupted me coldly. "There's not too much difference between one death and another," he said. "Nearly all of us end up suffocated." Then he straightened up in the chair that was a little too small for his size, as if reinvigorated. "Now let's forget about the housekeeper. Let's talk about your wife instead."

"About Nora? Why?"

THE SCARECROW

If it weren't for my wife's aptitude
for phone conversations, the heroic
methodicalness with which she
makes the rounds, each week, of
friends and acquaintances, giving
each one the time and attention he
deserves, we would not have heard
much about Mrs. A. starting that
spring. In fact, if it weren't for
Nora and her devotion to the telephone, a lot of things would not
have happened: we two, for example, would not have fallen in

love.

The impatient guy I used to be couldn't keep up any dialogue that wasn't face-to-face for more than a few minutes: I was dismissive, not inclined to chat, and I always had something in front of me that demanded my attention, usually a page of notes. My friends knew this, being programmed approximately the same way, so communication between us usually took place via brief text messages or a few lines via e-mail. By age twenty I had gained a questionable reputation for being rude to a classmate who had a crush on me, a girl I even liked. Every afternoon she called me on the phone for no particular reason, just to chat, she said. One day I had the guts to tell her not to call me anymore, because, unlike her, maybe, I had more important things to do. Wouldn't it be better to see each other at the university or when we had a date? Couldn't she do me a favor and hold whatever interesting thing she had to tell me until break time the next morning?

Nora had managed to turn all this around. The amount of time I spent on the phone with her had quickly aroused the suspicion — scary and disturbing — that something unprecedented was happening: to me, to her, to the two of us together. No matter where I was or with whom, I managed to find time to talk with her, unceremoniously leaving other people and obligations behind. At the end of every call, I checked the usage counter on the screen and was amazed at the lack of remorse I felt and, on the contrary, at the urge I had to redial her number. I have a sequence of recollections of myself walking around in circles, looking down at my feet, mostly listening to Nora and her pauses, while my earlobe overheated, pressed against the device's tiny speaker, and the palm of my hand sweated a little. She still teases me about how I was before I met her, and I doubt she will ever stop. "When I think about where I found you," she says, "in that hidey-hole where you'd retreated, all rigid and terrified, together with your quarks." For me, I suppose, falling in love will always be something akin to being flushed out.

In May, Nora, in a voice that's bright and chirpy (though too loud, exasperating me and making me ask her to lower it), uses the same Socratic skill she used with me to draw our unsociable, battered Mrs. A. into the futile conversations like those of the past. The remission period has arrived punctually for her, like every other codified stage of the illness. The magical disappearance of symptoms, all symptoms, including those related to the toxicity of the chemotherapy, has revived her interest in the world that still exists outside her body.

And so here come the horoscopes again, the pearls of wisdom summarized into pithy proverbs, the in-depth dissertations on how best to cook the zucchini that are just starting to flood the market stalls (yes, that's right, even her appetite has reawakened, what joy!) — in short, here is Babette, the woman we know and love, the rock we all lean on, who has no one to lean on in turn.

Occasionally dozing off, I listen to Nora, who is listening to Mrs. A. It's Saturday morning, past ten, but we're still lingering in bed as Emanuele busies himself in his room, making more noise than necessary to attract our attention. Getting some rest has put us in an easygoing, generous mood, appropriately sympathetic. While Mrs. A. fills Nora in on the cancer's remission, the hair that is growing back faster than expected (a little thinner than before and surprisingly darker, some of it actually brown), I wonder if she knows that her refound paradise is a classic stage, a temporary reprieve, ephemeral and somewhat sadistic, which represents nothing more than the classic approach to the final abyss.

She betrays some awareness of it only toward the end of the conversation, when, in a burst of enthusiasm, Nora asks her if she feels ready to resume caring for the vegetable garden now that she has her strength back.

"Oh, no, not the garden," she backpedals quickly. "I'm too weak for that."

They hang up after a moment, the sour aftertaste of misgiving in their mouths.

Nevertheless, the deeply rooted good sense with which Mrs. A. is equipped dictates that she live the final period of well-being as if it will never end. Fortunately, Emanuele's performance falls right within those two months or so of improvement. He has been chosen to play the somewhat unseemly role of the scarecrow in *The Wizard of Oz,* a leading role that Nora takes more pride in than he does; he would have preferred the part of the lion with the regal red mane.

We leave the making of the costume to Mrs. A. She still has admirable dexterity, and her hand is steady when she searches for the eye of the needle with the saliva-moistened thread. The result of an afternoon's work is impressive: she sewed patches on a pair of torn overalls, made one of my shirts into a jacket, and embellished them — along with a pair of boots that we had to buy — with strands of yellow yarn, to simulate bits of straw. When he puts on the costume, Emanuele hops around her, hands on his hips, like a sprightly imp, and for a few minutes they are again lost in each other. That will be our son's last private performance for his adoring nanny, who is captivated. I'm tempted to reach for my phone and take a picture, but I know that the balance of the moment is fragile and I don't want to disturb it.

The play, in fact, turns out to be very different from its domestic prelude. The unexpected attendance of all the members of Nora's family creates an emotional snarl-up during the long wait for the thing to start. The grandparents have gotten all dressed up as if for a gala evening — Nora's mother in a showy evening gown, her first husband and the current one in two curiously similar herringbone jackets — and now they all seem annoyed to find themselves in the bare foyer of an elementary school, among dozens of parents in jeans and short sleeves. They expect me and Nora to do something, find them chairs appropriate to their clothing, get them something to drink or at least come up with some way to entertain them.

Further, the gym where the show is staged turns out to be too small to accommodate this unruly crowd of relatives. Antonio, the second husband, wanting to impress everyone with his photographic equipment, complete with tripod and white reflective panel, argues heatedly with a man who, he maintains, is in his frame and who eventually tells him rudely what he can do with his panel. Mrs. A., being short, has her view blocked by a solid wall of backs and jackets. She, too, gives us disappointed looks, but we ourselves can hardly see the stage, which is not the least bit elevated off the floor, and we can't help her. The oppressive, stale air and the waiting on her feet make her dizzy. A woman holds her up, then fans her with a sheet of paper. Before the end of the play, even before her adopted grandson has appeared onstage, Mrs. A. elbows her way through the crowd and leaves.

On the way out, Emanuele immediately asks for her. "Where's Babette?"

"She didn't feel well, but she saw the whole thing, and she said you did a great job."

His shoulders curve and his face

takes on such a dejected expression that I wonder if he's still acting a little or if a tiny piece of his heart has indeed just been ripped off.

The exaggerated praise of his various grandparents is not enough to raise his spirits. On the streaked linoleum of the gym, Emanuele had performed especially for Mrs. A. and for the two of us, but his happiness is not equivalent to two-thirds of that hoped-for total, because her absence counts more than our presence.

We quickly extricate ourselves from the good-byes and walk home, just the three of us: two parents and a small, sad scarecrow who doesn't let go of our hands until we reach the door; as if to say he gets it, he understands that people leave, people just go away, forever, but not us, he won't allow us to, not so long as he keeps us together like that.

The Black and
the Silver

Every child is also an extraordinary seismograph. Emanuele understood it before we did; he felt the shock wave that was approaching, and that's why he clung to our hands the evening of the performance. After Mrs. A.'s desertion, there had been a subterranean quake, a silent slippage of water tables and groundwater levels, and over the summer we would discover that the hypocenter of the disturbance was located in Nora's womb.

One morning, already dressed to go out, she announced that she was two weeks late. It didn't seem like news you would tell someone in a hurry like that, standing up, car keys in hand.

"Have you done the test?" I asked her, mainly to stall for time and transform my reaction into something preferable to confusion.

"No. I'd rather we first decide what to do about it."

"What to do about it?"

Nora sat down at the table where I had stopped sipping my coffee. She did not lean toward me, nor did she show any emotion when she recited the words she spoke right after that; she reeled them off like a paragraph committed to memory. "It's best if we talk about it now. I don't feel ready. I don't have the energy. I can barely manage the work I have to do and look after Emanuele. There is no one to help us, and you're always at the university. Plus, I don't think we'll have enough money, and to tell the truth . . ." Only then did she hesitate, almost as if the last words had slipped out of her mouth unintentionally.

"To tell the truth?"

"Things aren't going so well between us either."

I pushed away the place mat with the remains of breakfast. I had not had time to question how I felt about the news, but that wasn't the point: the point was how casually I was excluded from any real possibility of having a say in the decision, the abruptness with which Nora affirmed that our lives were, after all, separate. I tried to appear calm. "Nora, one chooses whether or not to have a first child, not the second. We're young, we're in good health, what would justify such an action?"

She thought about it for a moment. "That we're afraid. Too afraid. I am."

"It seems to me you've already made your decision. I don't know why you're even bothering to tell me about it," I said, and now my words sounded sarcastic, full of indignation.

She nodded without looking at

me, then stood up and walked out. She kept her face hidden from me. I'm almost certain that her endurance had been exhausted and that by then she was crying.

Oh, if Mrs. A. could have seen us in the weeks that followed! How disappointed she would have been. When Emanuele was nearly three years old, she had launched a personal campaign for us to give him a baby sister (she never even considered the possibility of a boy): a series of inconsequential pedagogical opinions suggested to her that there was a precise window of time within which to plan for another child.

"You have the room," she said, as

if that were the main obstacle.

We'd tease her. "Isn't one enough for you, Babette? In a while, maybe. Who knows?" In the meantime we procrastinated, disappointing her. Never would she have expected, however, that, faced with a fait accompli, Nora would dream of backing out.

But Mrs. A. was more unreachable than ever. Since the illness had advanced swiftly and steadily, around the middle of July she had moved to her cousin Marcella's house, where for the most part she would live out her last five months, lying on the right side of a double bed that wasn't hers. The cancer had breached another rampart and seized control of her brain as well.

Talking on the phone had become difficult — her voice was gone; to communicate with her, we had to go through the extraneous filter of Marcella, while to see her we had to ask permission and then be watched the whole time.

Nora wouldn't admit it, nor would she do so later on, but she was scared, terrified of the possibility of spending a second pregnancy in bed. The months of immobility with Emanuele had marked her more deeply than I had realized, and this time there would be no Mrs. A. by her side, only a harried husband in whom, I understood that summer, she did not have enough faith. From that day on, neither of us held anything back, baring resentments that had long been concealed, in a painful, relentless crescendo.

In the end Nora's lateness turned out to be a false alarm, but at that point it didn't matter much; the effects had already been felt. Outwardly our married life went along unchanged, structured around a sequence of commitments, yet as if its heart had been drained. I had seen Nora sad, upset, angry but never listless or indifferent. Without the intercession of her exuberance, the world went back to being the cold shell that I had inhabited before I met her. Even Emanuele, at times, appeared alien to me.

"We could eat at the fish place

tonight, talk a little."

"If you want. Though I'm not very hungry."

"Let's go anyway."

And then we sat there eating dinner like strangers, no different from those couples who have nothing to say to each other, whom we had often pitied from the pedestal of our rapt enthrallment.

"What's gotten into you?"

"Nothing."

"You look sad."

"I'm not sad, I'm just thinking."

"About what, then?"

"About nothing!"

"You're scaring me. Are you doing it on purpose?"

We continued needling each other, anything to break a silence for which we were unpracticed. Nothing seemed to come to our rescue: considering how foolishly we behaved, ours might have been the first marital crisis in the history of mankind.

A young couple can also fall ill, from insecurity, from routine, from isolation. Metastases flourish unseen, and ours soon reached the bed. For eleven weeks, the same period in which Mrs. A. was losing the elementary functions of her body one by one, Nora and I didn't touch or reach out to each other. Lying at a safe distance, our bodies seemed like impregnable slabs of marble.

Dozing lightly, I tortured myself thinking about the time when her body was available to me and mine to her, when I could caress her without asking permission, anywhere — on the neck, her breasts, between the curved notches of her spine, along the cleft of her buttocks — when I was free to slip my fingers under the elastic without worrying about annoying her and she, drowsy, would return my attentions with an instinctive shiver. Neither one of us refused sex, ever; we might neglect it for long periods of time due to lack of opportunity and energy, but we did not withhold it. No matter how things were going, we knew that an untarnished space awaited us in our bedroom, a refuge of furtive embraces and caresses.

If our cancer had also aimed to affect the brain, then it had succeeded: with my wife lying a few inches away, I no longer knew how to approach her. My memory of those days and nights is sketchy and contradictory, riddled with rancor and appalling fantasies in which Nora betrayed me with someone, anyone.

What Galen does not explain clearly is whether humors can be mixed together like paints or whether they coexist separately, like oil and water; he does not explain whether yellow produced by the liver combined with the red of blood creates a new orange-colored temperament, nor whether an exchange between individuals is possible, through contact, effusions or even pure sentiment. For a long time, I thought it was. I was sure that Nora's silver and my black were slowly blending together and that the same burnished metallic fluid would eventually course through both of us. Then, too, we were both convinced that Mrs. A.'s glowing lymph would add another nuance to our own, making us stronger.

I was wrong. We were wrong. Life sometimes narrows like a funnel, and the initial emulsion of the humors produces layers. Nora's exuberance and my melancholy; Mrs. A.'s viscous stability and my wife's ethereal disorder; the lucid mathematical reasoning that I had cultivated for years and Babette's intuitive way of thinking: each element, despite assiduousness and affection, remained discrete from the others. Mrs. A.'s cancer, a single, infinitesimal clot of unruly cells that had multiplied relentlessly before becoming evident, had called attention to our separateness. We were, in spite of our hopes, insoluble in one another.

BIRD OF PARADISE
(II)

There are progressions whose epilogue is written in the prologue.
Did anyone, including Mrs. A.,
even for a minute think that things
could go any differently than they
did? Did anyone ever mention the
word "cure" to her? No, never. At
most we said that things would get
better, but we didn't believe that
either. Her decline was wholly
inscribed in the pulmonary shadow
etched on the first thoracic plate.
All these cancer stories are the

same. Maybe. That doesn't mean that her life wasn't unique, deserving of a story all its own; until the very last moment, her life was worthy of the hope that fate might make an exception for her: special treatment in exchange for the services she had rendered to so many.

The way things were between us after the summer, Nora and I had no thought for anyone else. It was one of Mrs. A.'s cousins who called us on a day in late November. "She wants to see you. I don't think she will last much longer."

We discussed whether we should bring Emanuele with us. I argued yes, that it made no sense to deprive a child of the sight of suffering, and besides, he was big enough to handle it. But Nora didn't want the image of Mrs. A. dying to wipe out all the other memories.

She was right. All that remained of Babette, under the many layers of blankets in the strange bed, was a shrunken, gray form. The room was permeated with a sickly-sweet medicinal odor and something indefinable that, when I bent down to brush the skin of her cheek in a hesitant imitation of a kiss, I found was coming from her lips: a whiff of fermentation, as if her body had already started dying from inside, one organ at a time. There was a strange light, shimmering and somewhat otherworldly, perhaps because of the gleaming elements that reflected it: the gold-

embroidered bedspread and trans-
lucent curtains, the gilt wardrobe
handles and brass fixtures.

As soon as she sat down on the
edge of the bed, Nora burst into
tears. I saw them again then, after
nine years, in the same roles as
before but reversed: Mrs. A. lying
down and my wife at her bedside.
She was trying to fasten a bracelet
around Babette's skeletal wrist, one
we had bought her so that she
might have a sign of us to accom-
pany her on her upcoming journey,
but Nora's fingers were trembling
and she kept missing the clasp.
Even in their reversed roles, it was
Mrs. A. who tried to console.
"Don't cry, Nora," she said, "don't
cry. For a while we were good

company for each other."

I left the room, closing the door behind me. Nora's tears had melted something inside me, unlocked a tenderness that had never gone away, and despite the tragic nature of the moment I felt an incongruous relief. We had bought some white tulips because they were Mrs. A.'s favorite flower and because showing up with assorted gifts seemed like an effective defense against the circumstances. Marcella looked for a vase, and I busied myself arranging the flowers in it after trimming the stems. I made an effort to keep up a conversation to prevent her from returning to the room where, I sensed, she would have liked to keep an eye on the situation, lest her cousin indulge in inappropriate confidences with my wife. I wanted to make sure Nora had all the private time she deserved.

When I went back to the bedroom, I placed the vase on the nightstand. There was a photo of Renato that I had seen elsewhere, taken in winter on the seaside promenade in Sanremo. Maybe thinking that he was waiting for her was enough to give Mrs. A. renewed strength, a strength that did not require flesh and bones or a voice.

"So, then, take care," I said to her.

She smiled at me. There was no need to pretend anymore. Death was already there among us, occupying the empty half of the bed, waiting quietly.

Mrs. A. was still gripping Nora's hand, or vice versa. "Look after her, always," she urged me.

"Of course. Always," I promised.

Nora turned slightly toward me, as if to say, "See how easy it is? Why couldn't you do it sooner?" I leaned over and kissed my wife on the temple.

"Now we'll let you rest," I said to Mrs. A., though she was already half asleep. Who knows where she found the energy to stay awake for those few minutes, which painkillers and tranquilizers she had struggled against, just to make sure that Nora and I swore we would go on taking care of each other.

We left her sleeping soundly. As I walked away from the room, I glanced toward the window. Through the lace curtains and double panes, I would not have been surprised to see an exotic bird with yellow and blue feathers and a long white cottony tail perched on the windowsill, its dark eyes, serious and compassionate, trained on all of us.

A few days later, Nora bought a perforated pan for roasting chestnuts. The metal was shiny and untarnished, very different from Mrs. A.'s battered, rust-covered one. Every autumn Babette had performed that ritual. She went looking for chestnuts in the woods behind her house, gathered them when they were still in the husk, then appeared at our place to roast them. I'd help her score them one by one, and that evening we would dine on chestnuts and milk sweetened with honey.

"They won't be as good as hers," Nora says. "They're from the supermarket. But let's give them a try."

As we eye the golden meats somewhat dubiously, she asks me to pour her some wine. "I thought I would switch schools for Emanuele," she announces.

"Oh?"

"Next year. They aren't doing enough for him where he is now. They don't understand him. She always said that. Besides, it's not right to tear up a child's paper."

"Teachers tear up papers. They always have."

"Not today. Today they don't do that anymore." She pauses to take a sip from the glass, then passes it to me. "I also thought that if they didn't renew your contract, it wouldn't be so bad."

"I think it would."

"It might be a good opportunity to try something different. Maybe elsewhere, for a while. I don't know." She puts a hand on my hip. "What do you think?"

"I don't know. It seems like such a lot of new things all at once."

"No. Here, take a look. Do you think they're done?"

■ ■ ■ ■

One night during her illness, Mrs. A. dreamed about Renato. It seldom happened that he came to her in her sleep. But that time he was standing in front of her, elegant as always, but with an incongruous felt hat pulled down over his head. He kept his hands shoved into his jacket and, not taking them out, gently invited her to follow him. "Come, it's time."

Mrs. A. was afraid he might be hiding something dangerous in his pockets, so she asked him to show her his palms. He ignored her. "Let's go, it's late," he repeated.

"I don't want to, not yet. Go away!"

Mrs. A. had backed away. Renato had bowed his head, disappointed. He'd turned around, and the darkness had swallowed him whole.

That night Babette had driven her husband away, despite her love for him: a fitting sign of her extraordinary attachment to life.

Around that same time I, too, had a dream. I was in a deserted underground parking garage. A shrub was growing from a crevice in the midst of the asphalt. When I went closer to look at it, I saw that the shrub was actually the majestic canopy of a tree, whose trunk descended several feet belowground, so far down that I could not make out its base. When I woke up, I associated that image with Mrs. A. —

but I never had a chance to tell her.

She belonged to that species of shrub that insinuates its roots into chinks in walls or cracks in sidewalks, that climbing variety for which an opening of just a few scintillas is sufficient to cling to, and then cover a building's façade. Mrs. A. was a weed, but one of the most noble ones. Even the mistakes she made in the final months of her life — giving up long before it was time, not preparing for the interminable future that would come after her, her dismay — were perhaps inevitable ones. There is no place for the thought of death in those who possess such an excess of life: I saw it in her, and I see it every day in Nora. The thought of death is only for those who are able to release their grip, for those who have already done so at least once. It's not even a thought, maybe more like a memory.

There was one thing she *had* provided for, however. Mrs. A. had made sure she had a place beside her husband's grave. There must have been a moment, an afternoon, perhaps, when she walked to the village cemetery clutching her black handbag, then from it extracting the cash to pay for the earthen bed that would receive her. I don't know if it took place before or after the cancer appeared, but I know for certain that even then it wasn't death's goading that drove her, but rather her love for Renato. She wouldn't have been able to stand being separated from him for another eternity.

"We should think about it, too," I said to Nora as we passed through the gate of the cemetery. I made believe I was joking, but I was serious.

"You always said you wanted to be cremated."

"Maybe I'm changing my mind."

She pursed her lips mischievously, as if to say that she would think about whether or not to keep me beside her all that time. Then she looked around, lost. "How are we going to find her?"

Since we hadn't followed the procession on the day of the funeral, we didn't know where

Mrs. A. was buried. One of the cousins had given my wife sketchy directions, which, considering her negligible aptitude for orientation, had become utterly useless.

"Earlier you said in back. Let's go try over there."

We divided up the aisles, as if it were a treasure hunt. Which, in a way, it was.

It was Emanuele who found her. "Come here! She's over here!" he shouted.

We ordered him to lower his voice, because it wasn't polite to yell in a place like that.

"But we're outside," he protested.

He was more at ease than we were among the dead. Afterward I thought that they couldn't help but be pleased to hear our son's crystalline voice, "a singer's voice," as Mrs. A. used to say.

The long white marble slab was clean, washed by rain or by someone who'd come by fairly recently. Emanuele climbed on top of it. Nora was about to stop him, but I held her back: she would have let him do it. He patted the color photograph of Mrs. A. and studied the one of Renato beside it uncertainly. "Ciao," he said.

Lying on the marble, tummy down, one ear pressed against the stone, he listened for quite some time. He was speaking to her in his mind, I think, because his lips were moving, though barely perceptibly. Then he got up on his knees and gave a sigh, a comical, somewhat affected sigh, like an adult.

Finally he spoke her name out loud: "Anna."

ABOUT THE AUTHOR

Paolo Giordano is the author of the critically acclaimed *The Human Body* and the international bestseller *The Solitude of Prime Numbers*, which has been translated into more than forty languages. He is the youngest ever winner of Italy's prestigious literary award, the Premio Strega. Giordano has a PhD in particle physics and is now a full-time writer. He lives in Italy. This is his third novel.

The employees of Thorndike Press hope you have enjoyed this Large Print book. All our Thorndike, Wheeler, and Kennebec Large Print titles are designed for easy reading, and all our books are made to last. Other Thorndike Press Large Print books are available at your library, through selected bookstores, or directly from us.

For information about titles, please call:
   (800) 223-1244

or visit our Web site at:
   http://gale.cengage.com/thorndike

To share your comments, please write:
   Publisher
   Thorndike Press
   10 Water St., Suite 310
   Waterville, ME 04901